"Mr Aguilar..." she began.

He raised an eyebrow. "Marco," he corrected gently.

Her incandescent summer-blue gaze slid away for a moment. He saw her take a deeper breath, as if to centre herself.

"I was wondering if you'd made a decision about whether you might be able to help the children or not?"

Marco took a few moments to marshal his thoughts. He hadn't embellished the truth when he'd told her at their first meeting that there were many charities he supported. Yet none of them was directly helping orphaned children. The subject was apt to bring back memories of a childhood he had striven hard not just to forget but to *hide* from the world at large.

"In truth, Grace, I would like a bit more time to give the matter some proper reflection before I decide. Is that all right with you?"

"Of course... It's just that..."

She leaned forward and he saw conflict in her eyes— maybe trying to press him for a decision was warring with her innate impulse to be polite. Even so, he wasn't above using whatever weapon he could from his personal armoury to get what *he* wanted. His success in business hadn't come about without a propensity to be single-mindedly ruthless from time to time. Pretty little Grace wanted something from him, and likewise he wanted something from *her*, he realised. He didn't doubt there was a way of gratifying *both* needs.

The day **Maggie Cox** saw the film version of *Wuthering Heights*, with a beautiful Merle Oberon and a very handsome Laurence Olivier, was the day she became hooked on romance. From that day onwards she spent a lot of time dreaming up her own romances, secretly hoping that one day she might become published and get paid for doing what she loved most! Now that her dream is being realised, she wakes up every morning and counts her blessings. She is married to a gorgeous man, and is the mother of two wonderful sons. Her two other great passions in life—besides her family and reading/writing—are music and films.

Recent titles by the same author:

THE LOST WIFE
THE BROODING STRANGER
ONE DESERT NIGHT

**Did you know these are also available as eBooks?
Visit www.millsandboon.co.uk**

A DEVILISHLY
DARK DEAL

BY
MAGGIE COX

First published in Great Britain 2012
by Mills & Boon, an imprint of Harlequin (UK) Limited.
Harlequin (UK) Limited, Eton House, 18-24 Paradise Road,
Richmond, Surrey TW9 1SR

© Maggie Cox 2012

ISBN: 978 0 263 22660 7

Harlequin's policy is to use papers that are natural, renewable
and recyclable products and made from wood grown in sustainable
forests. The logging and manufacturing process conform to the
legal environmental regulations of the country of origin.

Printed and bound in Great Britain
by CPI Antony Rowe, Chippenham, Wiltshire

A DEVILISHLY
DARK DEAL

Sheila, my romantic sister.
You had the best laugh and the most beautiful voice
and not a day goes by when my heart doesn't ache
because I miss them both so much.

CHAPTER ONE

Tipping up the brim of her wide straw hat, Grace Faulkner settled back in her deckchair, glanced through her over-large sunglasses at the glinting aquamarine ocean and sighed. She should be making the most of the tranquil scene and just relaxing, but it wasn't easy when her insides were deluged with querulous butterflies.

She was so besieged because very shortly she planned to confront one of this elite area's most revered and wealthy entrepreneurs and petition him to become a patron of the children's charity in Africa that was dearest to her heart. And not just to become a patron—but also to make a much needed generous donation so that essential building could commence on a new orphanage. The present one was all but being held up by hope and prayer alone.

What had fuelled her aim was hearing the owner of the café she'd been sitting in the day she'd heard the buzz that Marco Aguilar was visiting the area telling an American tourist that he'd known him as a young boy—that he'd grown up in a local orphanage and hadn't he done incredibly well for himself when you considered his start in life?

That overheard snippet had seemed more and more like divine providence to Grace as she'd mulled it over, and she didn't intend to let it go to waste. She knew she would probably only get the smallest window of opportunity to catch the businessman's eye before she'd be hauled off the premises by one of his security guards, and she should be prepared for that. But when it might mean the difference between helping to improve the lives of the children who had moved her so unbearably and returning to Africa with the news that she'd failed to secure them the funds they were so desperately in need of, a security guard trying to eject her seemed a small price to pay. Having recently seen for herself the squalor in which those orphans lived daily—a squalor that only the chance of a good education and caring patrons could help them out of—Grace had vowed to her charity worker friends before she left that she would do everything she could to help make that chance a reality. *But first they had to rebuild the children's home.*

The drowning noise of a helicopter coming in to land alerted her. *It had to be him.* Because she'd been so troubled and exhausted after her return from Africa, her parents had persuaded her to stay at their holiday home in the Algarve to take a much-needed break. For once she hadn't resisted their steering of her movements, and she was glad she had not—because on only her second day there she had heard the local buzz that Marco Aguilar was due to make a visit to one of his myriad exclusive hotels for a meeting. That particular hotel was situated in the resort complex right across the road from where she was staying, and if the rumours were at all to be relied upon *today* was the day. The arrival of the helicopter— the first she'd heard in three days at the resort—surely confirmed it?

With her heart pounding, she got up from the canvas chair positioned on the baking hot patio and quickly returned inside to the villa's pleasantly cool interior. Flying into the kitchen to grab a bottle of water from the refrigerator, she dropped it into her straw bag, repositioned her sunglasses on her nose, then pulled off her hat and threw it onto a nearby chair. Checking that she had her keys, she hurriedly left the building…

The helicopter had landed on a discreet pad somewhere amid the lush pine trees, and now there was a bank of sleek cars—mostly black—parked in front of the hotel. The impressive modern façade was edged by a pristine emerald lawn, and already there was a bevy of reporters and photographers running across it—a few that were ahead were moving swiftly through the revolving glass doors into the lobby. By the time the *mêlée* had disappeared into the hotel, and just as Grace was stealing a few apprehensive moments to decide what to do next, a gleaming black jaguar drew up at the front of the lawn. A burly cropped-haired bodyguard exited the car first then smartly stood holding the door wide as the man who was clearly his boss climbed out of the vehicle.

Due to his phenomenal success in business, and the purported enigmatic nature that was so indisputably appealing to admirers everywhere, photographs of Marco Aguilar were a regular feature in newspapers and magazines round the world, including the UK. There was no doubt that it was him.

Grace's first impression of the businessman that had made his fortune in the field of sports and leisure—in particular exclusive golfing resorts like this one—was that his physical presence was as commanding as his much-admired reputation. The impeccably stylish linen suit he wore was a perfect foil for his hard-muscled physique, and the moneyed air that radiated from the top of his shining black hair down to the tan-coloured Italian loafers he wore on his feet definitely suggested that the man had an unerring eye for the very best of everything. As he leaned over to speak to his bodyguard she saw even his eyes had the luxurious sheen of the finest dark chocolate. The sweltering Mediterranean sun was all but baking everything in sight, but in contrast he appeared ice-cool.

Narrowing her gaze to view him more clearly, she saw with trepidation that his hard jaw was undeniably clenched and the set of his well-cut lips formidably serious…perhaps even angry? Panicking slightly because if he was already ticked off about something then it was highly unlikely that he would even acknowledge her, she thought dismayed. Worse still, if he thought she was making a nuisance of herself he might call the police to arrest her.

Swallowing down her nerves, she tucked the leather strap of her straw bag neatly down by her side, then endeavoured to stroll casually towards the hotel entrance just as if she was a guest there—for surely this must be the window of opportunity she'd prayed for? It occurred to Grace that the reporters had made the mistake of assuming the VIP they so eagerly sought was already inside the hotel—perhaps smuggled in through a side entrance somewhere? Wishing that her heart wasn't beating so fast that she could scarcely hear herself think above the throbbing sound of it in her ears, she endeavoured to slow and deepen her breath to calm herself. *She had to do this.* The businessman's reputation and aura might be intimidating, but she couldn't let that stop her. Come what may, there was no backing out now.

'Mr Aguilar!' When she was about five feet away from him on the baking walkway she called out his name. The bodyguard immediately moved his intimidating bulk

Grace's way, to prevent her from getting any nearer. 'Mr Aguilar…please can I have just a moment of your time before you go inside to your meeting? I promise I won't keep you very long.'

'Mr Aguilar does not talk to anyone from the press unless it is prearranged.'

The bodyguard's heavily accented voice was a growl as he reached out to physically waylay her. She flinched as the man's huge hands encircled her bare arms in her sleeveless cotton dress, and at the same time saw a bead of sweat roll down his ample cheek.

His manhandling of her lit a furious spark of indignation inside her. 'Let me go! How dare you grab me like that? For your information, I'm not a reporter.'

'You have no business trying to talk to Mr Aguilar.'

'For goodness' sake—do I *look* like I pose any kind of threat to your boss?' Grace couldn't bite back her frustration. To get so close to the man she desperately needed to talk to and then be denied access to speak to him at the very last moment was *beyond* frustrating.

'Let her go, José.'

The man behind them snapped out a clear-voiced command and her heart hammered even harder beneath her ribs. The bodyguard immediately released his hold and she stepped to the side of him, at last coming face to face with her hard-jawed quarry.

'If you do not belong to that mercenary rabble from the press, who are primed to try and get me to answer questions about my private life and then embellish them for their undiscerning readership, what exactly *do* you want from me, Miss…?'

Indisputably his accent was Portuguese, but his English was close to perfect. The intensity of Marco Aguilar's examining gaze threw her for a second. The

rich caramel eyes with their fathomless depths seemed
to bewitch her. 'Faulkner...' she answered, her voice not
quite as steady as she would have liked. 'Grace Faulkner.
And, just to reassure you, I'm not remotely interested in
your private life, Mr Aguilar.'

'How refreshing' His remark was like a sardonic whip-
lash. He folded his arms.

Grace made herself press on regardless. 'I'm here because I'd like to tell you about an orphanage in Africa that
badly needs help...specifically *financial* help...to rebuild
the falling-down shack that houses it and to provide a
school and a teacher. I've recently come back from there,
and it's quite unbelievable how these poor children are
living—not even living... just existing. There's an open
sewer right outside where they're sleeping, and several
of them have already died from drinking contaminated
water. This is the twenty-first century for goodness' sake!
We're so rich in the west... Why are we allowing this to
go on without doing something more about it—without
every one of us feeling outraged on a daily basis?'

'I admire the passion and dedication you exhibit in the
name of your cause, Miss Faulkner, but I already give financial aid to several charities worldwide. Do you think
it fair to corner me like this when I'm about to go into
what is to me a very important meeting?'

Grace blinked. The rumour ran that he was there to
oversee the takeover bid of a less prosperous resort. It
was what he was known for excelling at...buying ailing
resorts and making them thrive, thereby reaping the benefits. If the newspapers and magazines were to be believed, the benefits aided his playboy lifestyle. *But how
much more money and power did the man need before
he decided enough was enough?*

Her indignation and temper got the better of her.

Pushing her fingers through the fall of blonde hair that glanced against her perspiring brow, she levelled her gaze with the billionaire's and didn't flinch even once. *'Fair?'* she echoed angrily. 'Do you think it's *fair* that these children are dying for want of even the most basic sanitation—and more importantly for want of love and care from the rest of humanity? Surely your "very important meeting" can't possibly be more important than that?'

In less than a heartbeat Marco Aguilar had positioned himself in front of her. The brief contraction in the side of his smooth cheekbone warned her that she'd struck a nerve. At the same time the sweltering heat that beat down on them from the dazzling sun up above seemed to magnify the hypnotic effect of his spicy cologne. Feeling a little bit more than slightly giddy beneath the twin onslaught of burning sun and aggrieved male, Grace wondered where she'd found the audacity—some might say *stupidity*—to imagine for even a moment that this was the way to get someone as wealthy and influential as him on her side. Clearly it *wasn't*.

'Let me give you a word of advice, Miss Faulkner... Please don't ever seek a career in a field that requires great diplomacy. I fear you would not get past the first round of interviews. You are very fortunate that I do not get my bodyguard to physically eject you from the complex. Forgive me...' the dark eyes swept mockingly down over her figure and up again to her face '...my guess is that you are *not* a guest here, are you? In which case you are already on dangerous ground, accosting me like this. Now, if you'll excuse me, I have a meeting to go to. My fellow attendees may not be as needy as your orphans, but I assure you they will be baying for my blood if I do not put in an appearance soon.'

'Look, I'm very sorry if I was rude to you, Mr

Aguilar... Honestly, I meant no offence.' Grace clamped even white teeth down on her lip for a second, in a bid to keep her passionate emotions under control, but it still didn't stop her from bursting out, 'All the same, you shouldn't sneer at my clothes and make me feel small in order to make yourself feel superior, should you? Besides, I'm not here to try to impress you. I'm here for one reason and one reason only: the orphaned children that I told you about. Yes, I *am* passionate about this cause, but I defy anyone *not* to be if they'd experienced what I experienced over the past few weeks. I really hoped you might help us...especially when I heard that you'd been raised in an orphanage yourself.'

The businessman stood stock-still and the bronze pigment in his skin seemed to bleed out and turn pale. 'Where did you hear that?' he asked, low voiced.

Her mouth dried. 'I heard it...just the other day.' Feeling almost faint with unease, and not wanting to incriminate the café-owner, she made herself lift her chin and not flinch from the steely-eyed glare in front of her, 'Is it true? *Are* you an orphan, Mr Aguilar?'

He exhaled a long sigh, as though to steady himself, then bemusedly shook his head. 'You say you are not a reporter, Miss Faulkner, but you attack your prey just like one. You must want what you want very badly to be so impertinent.'

'I do,' she admitted turning red. 'But only for the children...not for any gain for myself, I swear. And I didn't mean to be impertinent.'

Just when Grace thought she'd absolutely blown any chance of getting his help, and had started to regret being so bold, astoundingly, the businessman appeared to reconsider.

'Now is clearly not a convenient time for me to discuss

this matter further, Miss Faulkner, but you have sufficiently got my attention to make me consider a meeting with you at a later date.' Reaching into his inside jacket pocket, which she glimpsed was lined with light coffee-coloured silk, he withdrew a small black and gold card, extricated a pen as well, and scribbled something down on the blank space on the back of it. 'Give me a ring tomorrow at around midday and we will talk some more. But I warn you... If you tell anyone that we even had this conversation—and I mean *anyone*—then you can forget that you ever saw me, let alone hope to receive my assistance for your cause. By the way, what is the name of this charity that you so passionately support?'

Grace told him.

'Well... I will speak to you again soon, Miss Faulkner. Like I said, I will expect your call around midday tomorrow.'

Marco Aguilar turned and walked away, his faithful bodyguard hurrying after him and mopping his brow with his handkerchief as he endeavoured to keep up with his boss's long-legged stride. Gripping the card he'd given her as if it was the key to unlocking the secrets of the universe, Grace let her captive gaze ensure she followed the pair until they went through the hotel's entrance and disappeared inside...

Grateful for the almost too efficient air-conditioning in the luxuriously appointed boardroom, after the unforgiving midday heat outside, Marco restlessly flipped his gold pen several times between his fingers as he tried to focus on his company's earnest director, seated at the far end of the long mahogany table.

The loyal Joseph Simonson was being as meticulous and articulate as usual with his information about the takeover bid—the man's presentation couldn't be faulted—yet Marco found it difficult to pay proper attention to his opening speech because he couldn't get the memory of a pair of flashing brilliant blue eyes and a face that was as close to his imagined depiction of the mythical Aphrodite out of his mind.

Grace Faulkner.

But it wasn't just her beauty that had disturbed him. Marco wondered how she had learned that he had grown up in an orphanage when it wasn't something that he had ever willingly broadcast. A further conversation with her was imperative if he was to impress upon her the folly of repeating that information to the media—even though he knew there were local people who had always known it to be true. Perhaps he had been uncharacteristically foolish in hoping for their loyalty and believing they wouldn't talk about his past with outsiders? He'd already been through a torrid time with the press... The last thing he needed was some new revelation to hit the headlines. And this one would perhaps be the most difficult for him to face out of all of them.

His thoughts returned to the image of Grace Faulkner that seemed to be imprinted on his mind. She'd declared that she wasn't trying to impress him, but inexplicably she *had*. He'd already telephoned his secretary Martine and asked her to undertake some research on the woman and the charity she supported before he took her phone call tomorrow. *Unfortunately, it wouldn't be the first time that a female had behaved dishonourably to win herself the chance of getting close to him...accepted a fee from a newspaper for passing on some invented salacious anecdote about his life for them to print.*

Marco found himself wishing that the girl *was* unquestionably who she said she was, and that the only reason she had waylaid him *was* because she wanted his aid for the cause that was apparently so close to her heart. When he'd stood in front of her, so close that gazing into her eyes had been like being dazzled by a sunlit blue lake, she hadn't flinched or glanced guiltily away. No, she'd stared right back at him as if she had absolutely nothing to hide...as if she was telling him nothing but the truth. *What would she think if she knew how seductive and appealing that was?* He had dated and bedded some very beautiful women over the years, but their mostly self-seeking natures had *not* been beautiful.

Take his ex-girlfriend Jasmine, for example. The fashion model had made the mistake of trying to sue him for breach of his alleged promise to support her when the famous fashion house she'd modelled for hadn't renewed her contract because she'd preferred to party and get high rather than turn up for work. Marco had made no such promise to her...in fact he had already told her that he was ending their relationship *before* her illustrious employers had dropped her. The woman had been a liability, but thanks to his lawyers the case had been more or less thrown out of court for a laughable lack of evidence. Shortly after that sorry episode she had sold her lurid little tale to a tabloid for some ludicrous sum, inventing stories of 'ill treatment' and making him look like some despicable misogynist.

That whole sorry debacle had happened over six months ago now, and ever since then Marco had become even more wary and cynical of women's motives for seeing him. Despite his understandable caution, the fact that Grace Faulkner seemed far more interested in helping others instead of herself definitely made him want to find out more about the angelic-faced beauty, with a soft heart for needy children and the daring to just walk right up to him and present her case as if she had every right in the world to do just that...

'Marco?'

Joseph was looking decidedly ill at ease, because his boss hadn't replied to a question he'd asked, and Marco had the vague notion that he'd already addressed him twice. The rest of the board members shifted their gazes uncomfortably. Clearly they weren't accustomed to their illustrious leader being so distracted.

Folding his arms across the hand-tailored jacket of his cream linen suit, he allowed an apologetic smile to hijack his usually austere lips. 'Could you go over that again for me, Joseph? I think I must be a little jet-lagged after flying in from Sydney late last night and I didn't quite take it all in.' He shrugged.

'Of course.' At this amenable explanation, the British director's shoulders visibly relaxed. 'I'm sure that all of us here will endeavour to keep the meeting as short as possible in light of the fact that you must be understandably tired after your travels.'

With a little dip of his head Marco indicated his thanks, making sure to include every one of the well-dressed ensemble in his amicable gaze.

'By the way,' the other man added, his smile a little awkward, as if he were much happier dealing with matters appertaining to the business rather than making polite conversation with his boss, 'how does it feel to be back home? It must be at least a couple of years since you were here for any length of time?'

'That's right...it is.' His usual guard slammed down into place and Marco deliberately ignored the first part of the question. *Home was a concept that even his immense wealth had never been able to make a reality for him.* When a man had grown up an orphan, as he had, 'home' was just a tantalising dream that was always mockingly out of reach…a fantasy that just wasn't on the agenda, no matter how much his heart might ache for it to be possible…

A palatial house or mansion didn't equal a home in the true sense of the word, although he had several of those round the globe. Lately he'd been working particularly hard, and his plan had been to stay in the Algarve for a few weeks at least, to kick back and take a long overdue rest, but the instant he had recalled his humble beginnings growing up Portugal, the idea suddenly lost most of its appeal. The prospect of spending time alone didn't sit well with him either. Marco had plenty of acquaintances, but no real friends he could truly be himself around… *Even as a child he had never made friends easily.* One of the carers at the orphanage had once told him he was a 'complicated' little boy. With his child's logic, he had judged that to mean that he was difficult to love…

Once more he flipped his pen, hating the sudden prickling of anxiety at the back of his neck and inside his chest—a sign that he was feeling hemmed in, almost *trapped.* Because for him there was neither solace nor reassurance in revisiting scenes from his past.

'Let's continue, shall we? I'm sure we are all very busy people with much to accomplish before the day is out, and time is not standing still,' he announced abruptly.

Grimacing in embarrassment at his boss's terse-voiced remarks, Joseph Simonson shuffled the sheaf of papers in front of him and cleared his throat before proceeding…

Grace's insides were churning. It was a minute or two away from midday, and three times now she had snatched her shaking hand away from the telephone. Right then the fact that she might be just a conversation away from getting the financial assistance the charity needed to rebuild the children's home, set up a school and employ a teacher, didn't seem to help overcome her nerves. Yesterday she'd been fired up...*brave*...as if neither man nor mountain could stop her from fulfilling her aim of getting what she wanted. Today, after a more or less sleepless night when memories of Marco Aguilar's piercing dark eyes had frequently disturbed her, she didn't feel capable of much...let alone feel brave.

'Oh, for goodness' sake!'

Exasperated, she grabbed the receiver from its rest on the kitchen wall and punched out the number she had determinedly memorized, in case by some cruel twist of fate she lost the card.

On arriving back at the villa yesterday afternoon, Grace had been seriously taken aback when she'd realised the number Marco had given her belonged to his personal mobile. It wasn't the same as any of the numbers printed in gold on the front of his business card. Now, briefly shutting her eyes, she recalled the shining hopeful faces of the children she had left behind in that feebly constructed orphanage back in Africa and felt a resurgence of passion for helping make things right for them. *Marco Aguilar was only a man.* He was made of flesh and blood and bone, just as she was, she told herself. It didn't matter that he wore hand-tailored suits that probably cost the earth, or that he might regularly make it onto the world's rich lists. *That didn't make him any better than Grace.* In this instance they were just two humane people, discussing what needed to be done to help those less fortunate than they were, and she would hold onto that thought when they spoke.

The softly purring ringtone in her ear ceased, indicating someone had picked up at the other end.

'Olá?'
'Olá.'
'Mr Aguilar?'
'Ah…is that you, Grace?'

She hadn't expected him to address her by her first name, and the sound of it spoken in his highly arresting, accented voice made her insides execute a disorientating cartwheel. Staring out of the opened windows at the sun-baked patio, and the usually inviting deckchair that she'd had to vacate when the heat grew too intense to bear comfortably, Grace nervously smoothed her palm down over the hip of her white linen trousers.

'Yes, it's me. I presume I'm talking to Marco Aguilar?'
'Just Marco is fine.'
'I wouldn't presume to—'

'I am inviting you to address me by my first name, Grace, so you are not being presumptuous. How are you today? I trust you are enjoying this glorious weather?'

'I'm…I'm fine, and, yes I am enjoying the weather.' Threading her fingers through her wheat-coloured hair, Grace grimaced, taken aback that he should address her so amicably and not quite sure about how to proceed. 'How are you?' she asked cautiously.

'I wasn't planning on making this conversation *that* long,' he commented wryly.

Colouring hotly, she was glad that he couldn't see her face right then…just in case he imagined that she was one of those starstruck women who didn't have the wits to separate fantasy from reality…

'Well, I know you must be a very busy man, so you needn't worry that I'll talk your ears off.' She made a face, thinking that she sounded like some immature schoolgirl with that infantile remark. 'I promise,' she added quickly, as if to emphasise the point.

'Talk my ears off?' Marco echoed, chuckling, 'I hope you won't, Grace, because they are extremely useful at times…especially when I'm listening to Mozart or Beethoven.'

'I shouldn't have said that. It was a stupid comment.'

'Why? Because you think I might lack a sense of humour? I hope I may have the chance to prove you wrong about that.'

Taken aback once more by such a surprising remark, Grace hardly knew what to say.

'It may surprise you,' the man on the other end of the line continued, 'but I have unexpectedly found myself with an entirely free afternoon today. Instead of us talking on the phone, I could send my driver round to where you are staying and get him to bring you back to my house. That would be a much more agreeable way of conducting our conversation don't you think?'

She must be dreaming. Confronting him outside the exclusive resort was one thing, and talking to him on the phone was another…but never in her wildest dreams had she envisaged a man like Marco Aguilar inviting her to his house to discuss the charity she was so determined to help—just like that. If she didn't know better she'd think she was suffering from heatstroke!

'If you—if you really do have the time then, yes… I'm sure that would be a much better way to discuss the charity.'

'So you agree to allow my driver to pick you up and bring you back here?'

'I do. Thank you, Mr Aguilar.'

'Didn't I already tell you to call me Marco?' he answered, with a smile in his voice.

All Grace knew right then was that her parents would have a fit if they knew she was even considering going to a strange man's house in a foreign country in the middle of the day—even if that stranger *was* an internationally known entrepreneur. But then they were always so over-protective. She'd literally had to *steal* her freedom to leave home. Even when she'd made the decision to go to Africa to visit the children's charity she worked for in London she'd had to stand her ground with them...

'You can't keep me wrapped up in cotton-wool for ever, you know,' she'd argued. 'I'm twenty-five years old and I want to see some of the world for myself. I want to take risks and learn by my mistakes.'

'Grace?'

Frowning, and with her heart beating a rapid tattoo inside her chest, she realised that Marco Aguilar was waiting for her reply. 'I'm still here... I suppose I ought to give you my address if you're sending a car for me?'

'That would definitely be a good start,' he agreed.

CHAPTER TWO

THEY called them *casas antigas* in Portugal...manor-houses and stately homes. Grace's eyes widened more and more the further Marco's chauffeur Miguel drove them up the long sweeping drive that had met them the moment he'd pressed the remote device in the car to open the ornate electronic gates at the entrance. As they drove past the colonnade of tall trees lining the way she caught sight of the palatial colonial-style house they were heading towards, with its marble pillars glistening in the afternoon sunshine. She stared in near disbelief, murmuring, 'My God...' beneath her breath.

Inevitably she thought of the ramshackle building that housed the orphanage back in Africa, and was struck dumb by the heartbreaking comparison to the dazzling vision of nineteenth-century architecture she was gazing at now. Did Marco Aguilar live here all by himself? she wondered. Just the thought seemed preposterous.

The smiling chauffeur in his smartly pressed black trousers and pristine white shirt opened the Jaguar door at her side to let her out, and as Grace stepped down onto the gravel drive the scent of heady bougainvillaea mingled with the heat of the day to saturate her senses. Lifting her sunglasses up onto her head, she glanced back at the house and with a jolt of surprise saw Marco, standing on one of the wide curving upper steps, waiting. *'Olá!'* He raised a hand, acknowledging her with a brief wave.

He wore khaki-coloured chinos and a white T-shirt that highlighted his athletic, muscular torso, and his stance was much more at ease than when she'd seen him yesterday. Her trepidation at speaking with him again eased slightly…but only *slightly.*

When she reached the level just below where he stood, he held out his hand to warmly enfold her palm in his. He smiled. 'We meet again.'

His touch submerged Grace in a shockwave of heated sensation that rendered her unable to reply immediately.

This is terrible, she thought, panicking. *How am I supposed to sound at all competent and professional and say what I want to say if I'm completely thrown off-balance by a simple handshake?*

'Thanks for sending the car for me,' she managed. 'This is such a beautiful house.' Quickly retrieving her hand, she tried hard to make her smile relaxed to disguise her unexpectedly strong reaction to his touch.

'I agree. It is. Why don't you come inside and see it properly?' he invited.

If Grace had felt overwhelmed at the imposing façade of Marco's house, then she was rendered almost speechless by the opulence and beauty of the interior. A sea of marble floor and high intricate ceilings greeted her over and over again as her host led her through various reception rooms to what appeared to be a much less ostentatious and intimate drawing room. Elegant couches and armchairs encircled a large hand-knotted Persian rug in various exquisite shades of red, ochre and gold, whilst open French doors revealed a wide balcony overlooking landscaped gardens stretching right down to the sea.

This time it was the bewitching fragrance of honeysuckle drifting into the room that fell like soft summer rain onto Grace's already captivated senses. She was utterly enchanted.

'Do you want to sit outside on the balcony? I trust you are wearing suncream on that delicate pale skin of yours?'

'I'm well protected—and, yes…I would very much like to sit outside.'

Settling herself beneath a generously sized green and gold parasol in a comfortable rattan chair, Grace glanced out over the lush landscaped gardens in front of her and sighed. 'What an amazing view…your own private paradise on earth. I hope you regularly get to share it with your friends. It would be a crime not to. I bet you must really love living here?'

As he dropped down into a chair opposite her at the mosaic tiled table a myriad of differing emotions seemed to register on her host's handsome face and she didn't see *one* that reflected pleasure.

'Unfortunately I probably don't appreciate it as much as I should, seeing as I am not here very often,' he said.

'But you do originally come from here don't you…? From the Algarve I mean?' The impetuous question was out before she could check it, and straight away she saw that Marco was irked by it.

'Now you are sounding like one of those too-inquisitive reporters again. By the way…where did you hear that I'd grown up in an orphanage?'

Swallowing hard, Grace sensed hot colour suffuse her. 'I didn't hear it directly… I mean…the person who said it wasn't talking to me. I just happened to overhear a conversation he was having with someone else in a café I was sitting in.'

'So it was a local man?'

'Yes. He sounded very admiring about what you'd achieved...he wasn't being disrespectful in any way.'

'And when you heard that I was due to visit the Algarve, and that I was an orphan, you thought you would take the opportunity to petition my help for your orphans in Africa?'

'Yes...I'm sure you'd have done the same in my position.'

'Are you?'

Folding his arms, Marco looked to be pondering the assumption—not without a hint of sardonic humour, Grace noted.

'Perhaps I would and perhaps I wouldn't. Anyway, I think we should talk a little more in depth about what you came here for...get down to the details, hmm?'

'Of course.' Relieved that her admission about hearing a chance remark hadn't prejudiced him against talking to her some more, she lifted her gaze and forced herself to look straight back into the compelling hooded dark eyes. 'But I just want you to know that this isn't the sort of thing I do every day...spontaneously railroading someone like you into giving their help, I mean. When I'm working at the charity's office in London I have to be completely professional and adhere to strict rules. We either do a blanket mailshot of people likely to make donations, or once in a while I might get the chance to ring somebody who's known for being charitable and talk to them personally.'

'If you're being honest, then that makes a very welcome change.'

Marco considered her so intently for a moment that Grace all but forgot to breathe.

'Honesty I can deal with. Subterfuge is apt to make me angry.'

'I'm not a liar, Mr Aguilar, and neither am I trying to fool you in any way.'

'I believe you, Grace. I believe you are exactly who you say you are, and also the reason why you accosted me yesterday. Did you not think that I would check? So... That aside, tell me some more about this cause that makes you risk being apprehended to get to me—I would very much like to hear how you got involved in the first place. Why don't you start by telling me about that?'

She shouldn't have been surprised that he'd checked up on her, but all the same she *was*.

Immensely relieved that she had nothing to hide, Grace told him about finishing her studies at university and still being unsure about what career she wanted to take up. Then she told him about a conversation she'd had with a friend of her parents whose son had been giving up his post at a children's charity in London to travel a bit and see the world. That family friend had suggested she apply for the post. As luck had had it, she'd done well at the interview and got the job. Grace had been there for a couple of years when the opportunity had arisen for her to go out to Africa and visit one of the many orphanages the charity was endeavouring to assist. She had visited several times since, but that first visit had changed her life, she told Marco, feeling a renewed rush of the zeal that gripped her to personally try and do something about the heartrending plight of the children she'd witnessed.

As she finished speaking, with hope travelling to the highest peaks one minute as she believed she might elicit Marco's help, then plummeting down the slopes of anxiety the next in fear that he might refuse her, Grace heard nothing but the sound of her own quickened breath as she waited for his response.

The sun's burning heat seemed to intensify just then—even beneath the wide umbrella that provided shade for them. A slippery trickle of sweat ran down between her breasts inside the silky white camisole she wore, and unthinkingly she touched her fingertips to the spot to wipe it away. When she glanced up again she saw an expression in Marco's eyes that was so akin to naked desire that she froze, her heartbeat slowing to a deep, heavy thud inside her chest and a carnal longing so acute invading her that the power of it made her feel quite faint...

Her soft voice had died away to silence, but more than a little transfixed Marco found himself helplessly staring at the sight of Grace's slender fingers moving to the neckline of her camisole. Diverted from her explanation about how she'd become involved with the charity, he'd already tracked the little bead of sweat that had slithered down from the base of her throat, and when he saw her dip her fingers inside the plain white silk underneath the small embroidered buttons to deal with it he was gripped by an all-consuming lust so blazing that it turned him instantly hard. His desire was fuelled even further by his conviction that her action had been totally innocent and unconscious.

Grace Faulkner was already making his heart race faster than it had done with any other woman whose company he'd shared in a long, long time, and he realised that he wasn't in a hurry for her to leave him any time soon.

'Would you like something to drink?' he asked, getting abruptly to his feet. At his guest's hesitant nod, he started to move back towards the open French doors. 'What will it be? A glass of wine? Lemonade or some fruit juice, perhaps?'

'A glass of lemonade would be perfect…thank you.'

'I will go and find my housekeeper.'

When he returned from the kitchen, where he'd arranged for their drinks to be brought out to them by
Inês—a local woman he had hired as housekeeper and
cook—Marco returned to the balcony, feeling a little
more in control of the fierce attraction his pretty guest
had unwittingly provoked. Yet his pulse still raced at the
sight of her sitting quietly beneath the parasol. With her
pale blonde hair lying softly against her shoulders, even
her profile was angelic. He privately confessed he would
do almost *anything* to get her to stay with him for the rest
of the afternoon.

Her smile was shy and a little reticent as he sat down
again. He had the sense that when she wasn't champi-
oning a cause she was the quiet, reflective sort. *He liked
that.* It would be a refreshing change from the women he
usually dated…all spiky demands and too-high expectations of where a relationship with him might lead.

'Our drinks will be along shortly,' he told her.

'Mr Aguilar…' she began.

He raised an eyebrow. 'Marco,' he corrected gently.

Her incandescent summer-blue gaze slid away for a
moment. He saw her take down a deeper breath, as if to
centre herself.

'I was wondering if you'd made a decision about
whether you might be able to help the children or not?'

He took a few moments to marshal his thoughts. He
hadn't embellished the truth when he'd told Grace at their
first meeting that there were many charities he supported,
and there were quite a few children's charities amongst
them. Yet none of them was directly helping orphaned
children. The subject was apt to bring back memories of
a childhood that he had striven hard not just to forget but

to *hide* from the world at large. Perhaps he had subconsciously aimed to dissociate himself from that quarter entirely in case it brought forth more intrusive and uncomfortable questions from the media about his past?

'I have no doubt that your children's cause is one that a wealthy man like me ought to readily support, Grace, and while I am definitely not averse to making a donation, having listened and talked to you, I would like a bit more time to reflect on what level of help I can give. If you leave the details with me I will look over them at my leisure and get back to you. Is that all right with you?'

'Of course...and it's fantastic that you've decided to help us. It's just that...'

She leaned forward and he saw conflict in her eyes—maybe at trying to press him to take action sooner rather than later, which warred with her innate impulse to be polite. Even so, he wasn't above using whatever weapon he could from his personal armoury to get what *he* wanted. His success in business hadn't come about without a propensity to be single-mindedly ruthless from time to time. Pretty little Grace wanted something from him, and likewise he wanted something from *her*, he realised. He didn't doubt there had to be a way of gratifying *both* needs.

'It's just that I don't want to take up any more of your time than necessary,' she said in a rush. 'I know you must be an extremely busy man.'

'Are you in a hurry to leave?'

'Not at all, but...'

'Yes?'

'I really don't want to offend you, or perhaps bring back hurtful memories of your past, but I just want to paint a picture for you if I may? Can you imagine what it must be like not only to have to contend with being

be an orphan, with no mother or father to love you and
take care of you, but also to live in a dirty shack without
even the most basic amenities that most of us take for
granted? I don't mean to be pushy, I really don't, but the
sooner we can alleviate their dreadful living conditions
and put up a new more sanitary building, the better. For
that we desperately need financial help. So when you say
you'll look over the details at your leisure…do you have
any idea how long that might take?'

Inside his chest, Marco's heart was thundering. No,
he didn't have to imagine what it was like to grow up
without a mother or father to take care of him…not when
he'd personally experienced it, growing up in a children's
home where there had been about five or six children to
every carer. The sense of emotional deprivation it had
left him with would be with him for ever, and no amount
of money, career success or comfortable living would alleviate his underlying feelings of being isolated from the
rest of the world and certainly not as deserving of love
as other people.

*But at least the building he had lived in had been safe
and hygienic.* He abhorred the idea of innocent children
having to contend with the dreadful conditions Grace had
emphatically outlined to him, so he *would* be writing her
a cheque so that they could have their new building. But
he wouldn't be hurried.

'Whilst I am a compassionate man, Grace, I am first
and foremost a businessman, who is meticulous about
looking over the details of every transaction I make. I'm
afraid you are going to have to be a little more patient if
you want my help.'

'It's hard to be patient when you personally know the
children who are suffering,' she murmured, her cheeks
turning a delicate rose. 'You've checked out that I am

who I say I am, and that the charity I represent is absolutely legitimate, so why delay? I can assure you every penny of the money you give us will be accounted for, and you'll get a receipt for everything.'

'I am pleased to hear it, but if you knew how many worthy charities petition me for financial aid you would perhaps understand why I must take the appropriate time to discern who receives it and when.' He paused to bestow upon her a more concentrated glance. 'You're studying me as if you cannot understand my caution in writing you a cheque straight away? Maybe you think that because I clearly have the money I shouldn't hesitate to give it to your charity? Perhaps you believe that I should feel guilty about having so much? If that is so, then you should know that I worked hard from a very young age to have the success I have now. One thing is for sure… I did not grow up with a silver spoon in my mouth, and neither was good fortune handed to me on a plate.'

The woman sitting opposite him at the table bit down heavily on her plump lower lip and her glance suddenly became fixated on the mosaic-tiled tabletop. When she next looked up her lovely blue eyes were glistening, Marco saw.

'I'm so sorry. I had no right to rant at you about the situation. I get too passionate, that's the trouble. You've been nothing but hospitable and gracious, giving up your time to talk to me like this, offering your help, and now I've been unforgivably rude and presumptuous.'

'I don't believe for one moment that you meant to be discourteous. However, I am beginning to realise that underneath that angelic exterior I see before me there is a veritable *wildcat*.'

'Only when I see injustice and pain.'

'Ah… God knows there is enough of that in the world

to keep you busy for the rest of your life, no? But, tell me, was that the only reason you came to the Algarve, Grace? To see if you could petition my help for your charity?'

Tucking a strand of drifting fair hair behind her ear, she released a long, slow breath. 'No, it wasn't. I truly only thought of asking your help when I overheard that conversation in the café. I'm here because I'm having a bit of a break from work, since you ask. I'm afraid I returned from Africa feeling rather exhausted and a little low after my last visit there. The sights I've seen haunt me. Anyway, my parents have a holiday home here and they suggested I come out for a rest.'

'So you are, in effect, on holiday?'

Her big blue eyes visibly widened, as if she was taken aback by the mere idea. 'I suppose I am. Although the truth is I'm not very good at relaxing. After being in Africa and seeing the children at the orphanage I can't stop thinking about them and constantly wondering what else I can do to help.'

'So when you learned that I would be in the area for a meeting you were determined to try and talk to me?'

'Yes…I was.'

Helplessly, perhaps *inevitably*, Marco found himself warming to his refreshingly candid guest even more. 'Clearly your desire to assist those less fortunate than yourself drove you to risk something you perhaps would not ordinarily do. You must be possessed of an exceptionally kind heart, Grace.'

'You make it sound like it's something unusual. There are some wonderful people who work for the charity who are equally committed and devoted.'

Inês appeared through the elegant French doors with a tray of drinks. The plump Portuguese woman's smile was positively beatific when Grace warmly thanked her for the tall glass of lemonade, and right then Marco thought it would take a stone-hearted soul indeed *not* to respond similarly to this young woman's generous warm nature.

When the housekeeper had left them alone again, he took a long cool sip of his drink then leant back in his chair. 'I told you that I unexpectedly find myself with a free afternoon today? I think I would very much like you to spend the rest of it with me. We will start by going out to lunch.'

Grace was sure that most women finding themselves in her position right now with the arresting Marco Aguilar sitting opposite and declaring they would go out to lunch, would silently jump for joy at having such good fortune. But Grace *didn't* jump for joy. The situation was just too unreal to be believable, and she didn't feel anywhere near equipped to go out to lunch with such a man. *Especially when she'd probably just offended him with her passionate outburst and more or less telling him he should help the charity.*

He was a successful and wealthy man, yes. But she'd learned that he knew personally what it was like to be deprived and go without—*emotionally* at least—having been brought up an orphan himself. Why he wanted to be with her for even a minute longer bewildered her. And if she *did* agree to go to lunch with him, what could she talk about? Save helping the orphans and maybe complimenting him again on his beautiful house?

Before leaving home she'd led a more or less uneventful life. In fact, Grace hadn't felt as if she'd really experienced life at all until she'd stolen her freedom and permanently left home after returning from university. God knew she loved her parents…was grateful for all that they'd done for her…but in truth there were times when their protectiveness all but suffocated her. They were always so afraid she'd make the wrong choices, always wanting to protect her from the possibility of making mistakes.

That was why she'd never felt able to tell them that she'd once briefly dated a man who had hit her in a drunken rage and tried to rape her. He'd never got the chance to hurt her a second time, but the psychological wounds he'd left her with had not easily nor quickly abated. Though she would never regret her decision to break free, that experience had made her wary of getting involved with anyone again. Even a so-called simple date seemed fraught with danger now.

'It's very kind of you to offer to take me to lunch, but... don't you have someone else you'd rather go with?'

Looking honestly bewildered, her companion shook his head—as if not quite believing what he'd just heard. 'In answer to that strange question I will only say that I would rather go to lunch with *you,* Grace. I wouldn't have suggested it otherwise.'

'But you hardly know me—and I hardly know you.' Tearing her glance free from Marco's disturbingly frank examination, she stared out at the sublime vista of shimmering verdant green that stretched out like an infinite plateau in front of them. It might as well have been a vast ocean and she a small rudderless boat lost in the middle of it, she thought. That was how vulnerable and afraid she suddenly felt.

'And how will we *get* to know each other if we don't spend some time together?'

As if to prompt her into making a decision, pangs of genuine hunger registered inside Grace. She'd been so keyed up about meeting with Marco again that she hadn't been able even to contemplate eating breakfast. *What harm could it do simply to have lunch with him?* In fact it would seem ill-mannered *not* to in light of him agree-ing to help the charity.

She proffered an uncertain smile. 'All right, then. I accept your offer...thank you.'

Already extracting his mobile phone from a back pocket, her host flashed a disarming grin. A grin that could melt a girl's insides at fifty paces... 'I know the perfect restaurant,' he said.

Another worrying thought seized her—one that she was nervous of drawing attention to. 'Is it the kind of place where you have to dress up?' she asked.

Marco's glance made a leisurely reconnaissance of her face, neck and shoulders. Her blood started to heat the second she drew his gaze. 'You don't have to worry about that when you're with me, *meu querida*. Besides... your beauty would grace *any* establishment. It matters not what you are wearing.' His smile became even more seductive. 'However...what you have on is extremely be-coming.'

'Even if I'm not up to the standard of your usual guests?' she quipped daringly.

'I am sorry I said what I said to you yesterday about your clothes. It was not the behaviour of a gentleman.'

'But now that you've apologised I promise I won't hold it against you.'

Even as he frowned thoughtfully at this response, Grace's lips were forming an unrepentantly teasing grin...

Marco's chauffeur drove them to a three-storeyed restau-rant that overlooked the ocean. As they walked up the winding path to the entrance a small group of staff were waiting to greet them—just as if the handsome busi-nessman was someone whose presence lit up their day.

They apologised profusely that the manager was away attending his daughter's wedding and couldn't be there to welcome Marco and his guest personally.

Her companion had a friendly word with all of them, Grace noticed, acting as if he had all the time in the world to spare. As she watched him effortlessly interact, she reflected on how different he seemed from the way the press depicted him. She hadn't read a great deal about him, but what she'd read definitely painted him as some kind of playboy, intent on enjoying the fruits his wealth and status had brought him to the maximum. But now, with the palm of his hand pressed lightly against her back, a more immediate realisation troubled her. The thin top she wore ensured that her spine was sizzling beneath his touch, just as though his fingertips had stroked over her naked skin.

A strange sense of *How on earth is this happening to me* assailed her as two of the attentive young waiters led them up the stairs onto the roof terrace.

The ambience was surprisingly intimate for what was quite a large space. As they were escorted to what was clearly the best table in the house, with a prime view of the matchless sunlit ocean, an equal fuss was made of both of them. Already in her mind Grace was calling it *the Marco effect*. Even if he hadn't been as well-known as he was, she didn't doubt he would draw attention— just like a sudden flash of dazzlingly bright light in a darkened room.

Having ordered their drinks, they were now on their own again—apart from the inquisitive glances of nearby diners, sneaking a look at her impossibly handsome companion every now and then that was...

Lowering the leather-bound menu he'd been given, Marco frowned. 'The emphasis is on seafood here. I should have asked if you were okay with that… If not, I am sure the chef can prepare something you would like more.'

Having glanced at the extensive menu herself, Grace realised again how ravenous she was. 'I love fish…in fact, I prefer it to meat. This restaurant was a good choice,' she reassured him.

'I bask in the light of your approval.'

'I wasn't being condescending. I'm just grateful that you brought me here. Look at the view—it's absolutely fantastic!'

'You don't need to feel grateful or deserving, Grace. The fact is I wanted your company. I want to get to know you better. Tell me…is there a boyfriend at home?'

She thought he was teasing her, and half expected to see his sculpted lips shape a gently mocking smile, but when she glanced back at him Marco's expression was quite deadly serious. 'I've been too busy to have a boyfriend,' she told him. Even though she tried not to let it, inevitably some defensiveness crept into her tone. Her fingers restlessly unfolded the starched linen napkin in front of her on the table, then folded it back again into its perfectly formed square.

'So there is no man to take you out to dinner or to the movies?'

It wasn't just this man's looks that were compelling—his deep, rich voice had its fair share of magic in it too. So much so that Grace was all but mesmerised by the sound of it. 'I have some good friends. If I want to go out to dinner or to a movie I go with them.'

She heard his quiet intake of breath and was transfixed by the indisputably intimate tenor of his beautiful dark eyes. 'And what about those other needs that a woman might want a man for?' he asked softly.

CHAPTER THREE

THOSE *needs* Marco referred to had been deliberately and carefully suppressed ever since that horrible evening when her then boyfriend, Chris, had flown into a dangerous rage because Grace had refused to give in to his demands to have sex. After accusing her of flirting with another man at the party they'd attended, he'd pushed her up against a wall and slapped her hard across the face. Just as she'd been reeling with the shocking ending to what had been a pleasant evening at a mutual friend's birthday party, he'd pinioned her to the floor, as if he would force her to give him what he wanted.

She had been beyond terrified. It was only when she'd made herself not give in to her fear and spoken in a quiet, reasonable tone, urging him to think about what he was doing and telling him he would bitterly regret it in the morning, when he was sober again, that he had seemed to come to his senses and let her go. She'd left him sleeping and never returned.

'The kind of needs you're referring to aren't that important to me,' she said now with a feeling that was a mixture of despair and dread settling in the pit of her stomach. 'They're certainly not as important as other things in my life.'

Leaning towards her across the table, Marco drove

every single thought out of her head when he gently caught hold of a blonde tendril of her hair and slowly entwined it round his finger.

'You mean like saving the orphans?' he suggested huskily.

Even as her blood heated, and the resultant intoxicating warmth drove away all traces of despair, out of the corner of her eye Grace registered the brief flash of a digital camera going off.

Her companion had registered it too. Unravelling her hair from round his finger, he rose smoothly from his seat and strode across the polished wooden floor to the smartly dressed male perpetrator, sitting across from them with his female companion. Without saying a word he removed the camera from the surprised man's hands, pressed what Grace was certain was the 'delete' button on the back, then calmly returned it.

Having obviously identified the couple as British, he declared, 'If you ever try and do that again I will sue you,' and only a fool would ignore the underlying fury in his tone. 'I see that your meal hasn't arrived yet. Take my advice: make your apologies to the *maître d'* and go and dine somewhere else.'

His point made, and frighteningly succinct, he returned to sit down again opposite Grace, not sparing the man he had warned so much as a single glance to see if he and his companion had taken his advice. Only seconds after he sat down again the couple had collected their things and swiftly exited the terrace.

'Does that sort of thing happen often?' Grace frowned.

The broad shoulders that his white T-shirt fitted so mouthwateringly snugly and that accentuated his strong toned musculature, lifted in a shrug. 'Often enough to be tedious,' he replied, a thread of weariness in his tone, 'but it will not spoil our lunch together because I will not let it.'

Even so, the intimacy that had hovered so tantalisingly between them before the man had foolishly snapped the picture had definitely disappeared. Grace told herself she should be pleased, but strangely…she *wasn't*. Now Marco's dark gaze was clouded with unease, and his shoulders looked tense despite his assertion that he wouldn't let the incident spoil their lunch. Suddenly she had a glimpse of how the downside of fame and celebrity must so heavily encroach upon the recipient's understandable desire for privacy. It made her partially regret her impulsive 'accosting' of him yesterday…

'Marco?' The distinct wariness in his returning glance upset her. 'If you would rather leave we can perhaps meet up again tomorrow instead? I know I pressed you about making the donation, and as far as the children are concerned it's definitely urgent, but I'm here for at least another week and a half.'

For the first time in longer than he could remember Marco had laid aside the demands and concerns of running a hugely successful enterprise for a while in order to give his full attention to something purely enjoyable for himself. This afternoon he had willingly surrendered his corporate persona to fully embrace the experience of being young and less careworn in Grace's refreshingly innocent company. But that thoughtless diner had tainted his pleasure, making him only too aware that he *wasn't* as carefree as he wanted to be. He'd had plans to enjoy a long, lazy lunch that could possibly extend into the evening. Now Grace had asked him if he would like to forego that and meet up tomorrow, or at a later date instead.

It wasn't an option he wanted to entertain even briefly.

The truth was he really liked the way this woman made him feel, and he craved more…*much* more of the feeling.

'I don't wish to leave, and nor do I want to postpone our lunch for another day.' As to if to highlight his intention, he snapped his fingers to attract the waiter hovering nearby, who had clearly been assigned to their table, 'I believe we are ready to order,' he announced, deliberately catching Grace's eye and smiling. 'Do you mind if I order for us both? If you like fish then I know the perfect dish. You will love it, I am sure.'

'Be my guest,' she replied quietly, her blue eyes flickering in surprise that he wished to stay after all. 'Go ahead and order.'

To accompany their meal he ordered a bottle of the very good light red wine the region was known for. Perhaps a glass or two would relax his pretty companion, he mused, thankfully sensing his previously less tense mood return. 'I am sorry if you were disturbed by that thoughtless idiot trying to take our picture,' he remarked. 'These people never seem to consider that I might need a private life as much as they do.'

'Having transgressed your privacy myself yesterday—albeit for the charity—I must admit I don't envy you, having to put up with that. It makes me realise that it's a great gift to be anonymous—to come and go wherever and whenever you please and to know that the public at large don't have a clue who you are and nor do they care.'

'You are fortunate indeed if you never crave the recognition of others to make you feel valued.'

The pale smooth brow in front of him creased concernedly. 'Do *you*?' she asked him bluntly.

Though no one would ever know it, Marco privately owned that sometimes he *did*. But he wasn't about to admit that to a woman he'd only just met. In fact, he wasn't going to admit it to *anyone*. It was a painful aspect of his ego that frustrated and irked him. But also perhaps inevitable that a man whose father had abandoned him to an orphanage as a baby because he couldn't take care of him on his own after Marco's mother died was fated to crave the recognition of others in a bid to help him feel worthwhile…

'Do I strike you as a man who courts the approval of others?' he answered, his tone a little more clipped than he'd meant it to be.

'I don't know. I've only just met you.'

Once again, Grace's luminous sky-blue gaze unsettled him, suggesting as it did that she intuited far more than was comfortable for him.

'But I imagine it's not easy to be in business in this world…especially if you have a high profile. It must be a lot like being an actor—you're always playing a role, and you can't really be yourself, can you? Especially when people believe that it's your success and reputation that defines you as a person. It must make it difficult to foster good relationships at work, and even in your private life.'

'So what have you personally heard about my reputation? I'm interested to know.'

The smooth space between her slim elegant brows crumpled a little, almost as though it grieved her that he should ask such a question. 'I don't read the newspapers very often, and when do I'm apt not to believe what they write about the lives of people in the public eye.'

'But nevertheless you *have* heard things about me somewhere along the line yes?'

'I've heard it said that nobody can be as successful as you are unless they're a little ruthless… But then they say that about a lot of successful businessmen, don't they?'

'Do you believe it? That I am ruthless I mean?'

'I trust that I'm intelligent enough to make up my own mind about a person. I certainly don't go blindly along with what the papers or the media says. And as far as thinking that you might be ruthless sometimes goes, I hardly know you well enough to form an opinion. But I do believe that the press has its own agenda, and I don't think it's got a lot to do with telling the truth. See what I mean? Everyone is playing a role…even journalists. Why isn't it enough to simply just be who you naturally are in this world? People are too afraid to let down their guard, that's the trouble. If they did, then they *would* be communicating authentically…but it's not something that's promoted in our culture.'

The waiter brought their wine and offered Marco a taste first. He took an experimental sip, pronounced it 'perfect' and waited for the man to pour some for Grace then leave again before commenting on her statement—a statement that had both shocked and surprised him with its insight.

'In business, to let down one's guard in front of the competition would be deemed corporate *suicide*,' he declared, at the same time wondering what she would have to say about that.

Lifting her hair briefly off the back of her neck, unwittingly drawing his attention to the graceful and seductive shape of her long, slim arms, she gifted him with a smile so charming that it made his stomach flip.

'Not if someone has faith in their own ability to make things work, no matter what the competition is doing. It seems to me that if you're not towed round by the nose by what your competitors think of you, then you're onto a winner…you're free to do whatever you like.'

The burst of laughter that left Marco's throat was

genuinely joyous—so much so that the other diners on the terrace couldn't stop themselves from smiling at the sound.

'I don't think I meant that remark to be funny.'

His lunch guest's pretty lips pursed a little, and she looked so adorable just then that Marco wanted to kiss her...wanted to obliterate every bit of her softly shaded pink lipstick and explore her mouth until time stood still. And even then he guessed that wouldn't be enough to satisfy his craving.

'I'm not mocking you, *namorado*...the exact opposite, to tell you the truth. You have no idea how refreshing it is to have someone genuinely tell you what they think. Sometimes it is hard to know who to trust because of the lack of that kind of honesty in my working life...even amongst my closest colleagues. Perhaps you ought to go into business yourself, Grace? You could spearhead a new trend for fostering good relationships and authenticity in the corporate world.'

'Now you *are* mocking me.' But even as she uttered the words the corners of her mouth were wrestling with a smile. 'I'm afraid I'm the last person in the world who should go into business. I'm neither clever nor ambitious. All I've ever wanted to do was to help people.'

'I don't believe you are not clever. You went to university and presumably got a degree, didn't you?'

'What if I did? Anyone can learn a bunch of facts and explain them in the way the system wants you to. That might be regarded as "clever" by some, but it doesn't mean that you're intelligent...at least not in the way that I understand the word.'

The waiters arrived with their meal right then, and Marco reflected that their arrival was most opportune—because the break in his and Grace's conversation allowed him some time to assess his feelings. The fact was, the more time he spent in this unusual and refreshing woman's company, the more her unsophisticated beauty and intelligence enthralled him, and his desire to take her to bed, to get to know her even *better*, intensified.

As the waiters once more left them alone, he raised his glass in a toast. *'Saúde.'* He smiled. 'Which means, to your health.'

'Cheers,' she answered shyly, touching her wine glass carefully to his...

He'd left her in the drawing room to go and talk to Inês about preparing dinner for them later on that evening. The feeling that she'd somehow stumbled into somebody else's dream continued to dog Grace. She'd eaten the most sublime lunch, been wined and dined at a beautiful restaurant overlooking the sea by a man whose photograph had probably appeared in every newspaper and style magazine worldwide, and even if she pinched herself she'd hardly believe it. Marco Aguilar was so charismatic and good-looking that she guessed a lot of women would even *pay* for the privilege to sit and admire him, just listen to him talk, simply because he was so mesmerising.

Less than halfway through their meal, the wine she'd imbibed heightened a worrying revelation: she was becoming more than a little attracted to him. Just the *idea* was enough to terrify her. Frankly, it was absurd. When they talked about people being 'poles apart' the description could so easily apply to Grace and Marco. There probably wasn't even *one* thing that they remotely had in common.

Now, relaxing on one of the elegant couches, with the still-hot sun beaming into the room through the open French doors, she could barely fight the fatigue that swept

over her, let alone resist her host's indisputable powers of
persuasion to stay longer and have dinner with him. She
really ought to get back to the villa, she thought sleepily. Clearly she wasn't quite recovered from the exhaustion that had hit her on returning from Africa. She had
to make the most of this holiday and rest properly. That
was why she should go *now*.

Making a half-hearted attempt to get up from the
couch, she slumped back down almost straight away—
because her legs just didn't seem to want to hold her up.
A few moments later her backless sandals slipped off her
feet as she dropped her head down onto the silk cushion
behind her and fell fast asleep…

'It's all right, little one I'm here now… I'll stay and
hold you until you fall asleep I promise…'

Her arms full of the warm weight of a baby, Grace
rubbed at the surge of hot tears that welled up in her eyes.
Every day when she visited the orphanage and saw the
mixture of sad and hopeful faces that waited to greet her
it became harder and harder for her to leave. *She'd become particularly fond of the baby boy that had been put
into her arms a few days ago, after his birth mother had
died of Aids.* Now on every visit she made a beeline for
him. *He was so easy to love. That was the most heartrending thing…* He deserved to have parents who adored
him. Surely there must be some kind couple in the area
who could adopt him and give him a home? *God, it was
so hot…* If she stayed here for another year she doubted
she'd ever get used to the enervating heat…

Opening her eyes, Grace shockingly registered that
she wasn't in fact in Africa, at the orphanage, but was
instead in the elegant high-ceilinged drawing room of
Marco Aguilar's home. She swung her legs to the floor,
pressed her hand to the side of her head because the

sudden movement had made her head spin then stared straight up into a pair of concerned dark-lashed brown eyes.

'I'm so sorry,' she murmured, beyond embarrassed and wishing that the ground would open up and swallow her. 'I don't know what came over me…falling asleep like that…a bit too much wine, I think.'

'You were dreaming,' Marco told her low-voiced. Dropping down with ease to his haunches, he reached out a hand to brush away the lock of hair that had tumbled onto her forehead. 'It was a dream that clearly distressed you. Would you like to tell me about it?'

'I thought I was back in Africa.' She tried for a smile, but her heart was bumping so hard beneath her ribs at his closeness that it turned into a grimace.

'It sounded as though you were comforting a child?'

'A baby,' Grace answered straight away. 'His name was Azizi—the helpers who work at the orphanage named him. It means beloved or precious one.'

The tight knot of tension that gathered inside his chest at her words made Marco rise to his feet again. He couldn't deny that he was touched by how genuinely loving she'd sounded about the baby…an infant that wasn't even her *own*. If only he had had someone even *half* as loving to look out for him as a child. It would have made a world of difference to him. He might not have grown up as emotionally detached as he had become…

One thing seemed clear: when Grace became a mother herself, her natural proclivity to be tender and loving would come into its own. Marco *envied* the man who would be the father of her children.

'If his destiny proves to live up to his name, then he will be a fortunate boy indeed,' he remarked, crossing the cool marble tiles to the opened French doors. Turning back to observe the pretty woman perched on the edge of his couch, her golden hair sexily mussed from her nap and one thin strap of her silk camisole sliding arrestingly down over one perfect satin shoulder, he folded his arms to try and contain the carnal heat that threatened to consume him. 'When I walked back in from the kitchen after talking to Inês I thought I had stumbled upon Sleeping Beauty,' he confessed. 'I should have pretended to be the handsome prince and kissed you awake.'

Her big blue eyes widened to saucers, then she sighed. 'But you didn't,' she uttered softly.

The throbbing heat that had already invaded Marco inflamed him even more, and he almost had to suppress a groan. 'Would you have liked me to?' he asked, his voice sounding like a hypnotised stranger's to his own ears.

Leaping suddenly to her feet, Grace hastily repositioned the silky spaghetti strap that had drifted down over one shoulder, then slipped her prettily arched feet into the sandals that were at the foot of the couch. 'I should go. It's probably not a good idea for me to stay for dinner after all. You've already taken me out to lunch and given up a lot of your valuable free time to be with me as it is.'

'You can't go,' Marco's reply was unequivocal. Already he knew that his house—this 'paradise on earth', as she had called it—would feel like a suffocating if luxurious prison without her presence this evening. She was more than just a breath of fresh air... she had him spellbound. And he scarce knew what to do with the torrent of feelings that were coursing through him. Never before had he experienced such an instantaneous and passionate attraction towards a woman practically on sight.

'What do you mean, I can't go?'

'I mean that Inês has already started to prepare the meal she is cooking for us tonight.'

'But we've only just got back from having lunch.' Running her hand over her hair, his guest lifted her wrist to examine her watch. She moved her head in stunned disbelief when she saw the time. 'It's just after seven o'clock... We left the restaurant at half past four. You don't mean to tell me that I've been asleep on your couch for nearly two hours?'

'You clearly needed to rest. In this part of the world it is not unusual to take a siesta after lunch.'

'You should have woken me...what must you think of me?'

It surprised him that she seemed so distressed. Most women would have taken the opportunity to maximise *any* chance to spend time with him...but not *Grace*. Accustomed to thinking on his feet, Marco moved towards her, circled his hands round her slim upper *arms* then smiled down into her upturned face with every ounce of the charm that newspapers and magazines regularly claimed he had. And not for an *instant* did he chastise himself for utilising that asset.

'It would have been a crime to wake you when you looked so peaceful. While I sat here and watched you I made the most of the time to reflect upon helping your charity and I'm pleased to tell you—rather than wait any longer—I've decided to write you a cheque tonight to pay for the new orphanage. To cover *all* the costs.'

'You mean to buy the land, purchase the materials *and* pay for the work to be done to build it?'

'That's what you wanted, wasn't it?'

'Yes, but I didn't expect you to— Oh, my God, that's wonderful! I could—I could *kiss* you!' Her cheeks flooded with the becoming colour of dewy pink roses even as her lips curved into the most bewitching sunny smile Marco had ever seen.

'You won't find me protesting about that,' he teased.

'But... You—you watched me sleep? Why?'

He lifted a shoulder in an unrepentant shrug. 'What do you expect a normal red-blooded male to do? Ignore the unexpected opportunity to gaze at such sublime beauty— undisturbed and at my leisure—when it was right here under my nose?' He stole a couple more seconds to look more deeply into her startled blue eyes before dropping his hands from her arms and stepping away...but not *too* far away. His palms tingled as if they'd been burned by the sun—just because he had touched her.

'Anyway...'

Unable to disguise her surprise—and also what he perceived to be her general awkwardness at what he'd just revealed—Grace linked her hands as if to steady herself.

'You really will write a cheque for the orphanage tonight?'

'I will indeed.'

'I can hardly believe it. You have no idea what this will mean to the children, and to the people who help care for them.'

'I think I do.' Helplessly remembering the long, empty days when he was growing up in the orphanage, craving love and attention and not getting it, he thought, *At least now I can do something to help another child growing up in similar circumstances to have a more comfortable and caring existence...* 'Why don't you come into my study and we will get our business over and done with before dinner?'

His smile enigmatic, Marco moved towards the door,

knowing that he had no qualms about the additional un-
conventional agreement he was going to propose as soon
as he wrote the cheque for Grace. None at all...

CHAPTER FOUR

IT WAS about an hour away from sunset, and the fiery orb still burned high and bright in the azure sky as Grace followed Marco through stunning marble halls into his study. In fact the light that beamed through the huge plate glass windows was so dazzling upon their entry that she squinted to protect her gaze. Her companion immediately pressed a button on a wall panel to lower stylish honey-coloured blinds, then gestured for her to sit down opposite him at the large beechwood desk that dominated the room.

Still feeling stunned that Marco was going to give the charity the help it so desperately needed to rebuild the orphanage, and anxious that at any time he might change his mind, she attempted to introduce some levity into the proceedings. 'I feel like I'm about to be interviewed for a post at one of your resorts.' She smiled. 'Would I pass muster do you think?'

'I only ever employ the very best people. If you are capable of rising to the challenge of doing an exemplary job then, yes…you would definitely stand a good chance of gaining a position in my company.'

The merest shadow of a smile touched lips that suddenly appeared austere, and Grace couldn't help feeling a little defensive at the idea her host might be privately questioning her ability and finding it wanting. All desire to lighten the mood fled. Was Marco subtly reminding her just who he was, and that she was lucky he'd agreed to talk to her at all about the charity—let alone invite her into his home? As soon as the thought entered her mind she gave herself an instant pep talk that she shouldn't be daunted by someone just because he was rich and well-known—she was sitting on the other side of his desk because her priorities, her ability *and* her heart were good. There was absolutely nothing she needed to feel 'less than' about.

He reached into a desk drawer, and she saw him withdraw a chequebook. Her heart started to thud a little. She caught her breath as she watched him write the name of the charity on the top line, then scrawl in an amount. Ripping out the cheque from the book, he turned it round so that it was facing her, then pushed it across the desk. The inside of her mouth turned dry as dust as Grace inclined her head to examine it.

'This much?' she exclaimed, hardly daring to believe the eye-popping amount on the cheque. 'It's at least triple the amount that we need. Why? Why have you decided to give us so much?'

The man at the other side of the desk finally let down his guard and smiled without inhibition. For the first time she noticed the crinkled laughter lines at the corners of his deep brown eyes. Now she was agog for an entirely different reason…

'As well as rebuilding the orphanage, this money is for the charity to do whatever it sees fit to help the children… Your passion and dedication to their cause, Grace, has helped bring it home to me how I have neglected the one area of need that I can personally identify with.'

He folded his arms over his muscular chest and briefly

glanced away, as though struggling with the memories that might still haunt him. Grace sensed her insides lurch sympathetically.

His arresting gaze returned to study her. 'The cheque is yours to take with you. However, there is something I would like to add before our transaction is concluded.'

About to pick up the cheque to examine it more closely, Grace stilled apprehensively. 'Oh? What's that? Is it perhaps that you want to go out to Africa to visit the orphanage and confirm what's needed for yourself? I'm sure the charity would be delighted to arrange—'

'I do not want to visit.' There was a hint of steel in his reply. Then he drove his fingers through his hair, as though frustrated that she should jump to that conclusion. He leant back in the impressive Chesterfield-style chair and exhaled a sigh. 'What I want is to make a personal arrangement with *you*, Grace.'

Her brow puckered. 'What kind of arrangement? You had better explain.'

'You told me that you have another week and a half left of your holiday?'

'That's right…'

'For the first time in quite a long while I find myself with the desire to take a sabbatical from work, and I would like to have an attractive and pleasant companion to join me for a while. If you agree to spend the remainder of your holiday with me, Grace, I will show you some of the finest private beaches, take you to eat at some of the best restaurants, and let you partake in any leisure activity you so desire. I have, of course, access to the most exclusive golf courses, if you're interested in learning how to play, and in the evenings if there is a performance somewhere we can go to a concert or a recital, perhaps? My personal preference is for classical music,

but I fully accept that you might prefer something else.'
Pausing, he lightly drummed his long, tanned fingers on
the desk, his glance honing in on her like a laser. 'All this
will, of course, be at my expense. Each morning I will
send a car to collect you and bring you back here. Once
you arrive we can discuss what we would like to do that
day. And there is one more thing…'

If she hadn't felt quite so numb with shock, Grace
would have pricked herself with a pin to convince herself that she still inhabited her physical body and wasn't
either hallucinating or dreaming. 'What's that?'

'I forgot to include shopping in the itinerary. I have
never met a woman yet who would not put that at the top
of her list of favourite things to do on holiday.'

'Well, you have now.' Shakily circling a small patch of
the desk with the tip of her forefinger, she couldn't help
but be affronted. 'It's never been top of any list for me
and never *will* be.'

'Hmm…' Marco's expression was definitely amused.
'Do you really expect me to believe you do not like beautiful clothes…exquisite jewellery?'

'Why would I pretend I'm not interested if it's the
truth?'

'Maybe you think you should play down such an interest? Who knows? There is no need. I am an extremely
wealthy man. The women who come into my life have
certain expectations. Clothes and jewellery are the very
least they expect.'

'What a shame.' A strong wave of compassion assailed
Grace as she thoughtfully digested this information and
observed him.

'What do you mean?' A shadow moved across his
piercing dark gaze.

'I mean it's a shame that women can't just like you for yourself…without you having to buy things for them.'

'Thankfully, I do not suffer with the same regret. I am a realist, if nothing else. And the truth is I do not indulge their love of beautiful clothes and expensive jewellery for *nothing*. I too have certain expectations—of them.'

Embarrassment at what he alluded to made Grace shift uncomfortably in her seat. But she was still genuinely sorry to learn that Marco must enter into such cold-blooded liaisons with women believing he had to pay for the privilege. She didn't doubt that it couldn't exactly make him feel very good about himself, for all his talk about being a realist. Inside, she guessed that the small boy he had once been was still searching for evidence that he was valued in some way, and maybe felt he always had to *give* something in order to get something back in return. It made her want to show him that he *was* valued and didn't need to deserve it. He was a good man. Grace was certain of that.

'That's all well and good,' she said, 'but I still think you're missing something important if a woman doesn't just want to be with you because she genuinely finds pleasure in your company and—and cares about you.'

He scowled. 'You are clearly a romantic, Grace, and not remotely a realist.'

'If realism means that people can't like me unless I give them something, then I'm glad I'm what you label a romantic. Look…please don't be offended by what I've said…' Her irked glance automatically softened. The last thing she wanted to do was alienate or wound him by expressing her perhaps *too* frank opinions. After all, she had utterly no experience of the kind of world Marco moved in, or the compromises and personal sacrifices he found himself having to make. 'It's just that the things I find most beautiful are all natural…a sunset over a green valley, a deserted sandy beach as dusk falls, a bluebell-carpeted wood or the scent of roses in an English country garden…the joy on the faces of children who are simply happy that an adult is paying them some real attention…'

Her avid listener sat up straight in his chair and a much more interested glint came into his eyes. 'If you genuinely prefer all those things then you are indeed a unique woman in our consumer-driven day and age.'

'I don't think so. If you haven't met other women like me it doesn't mean that they're not around. You just move in a very elite sphere where perhaps the women's focus is more on the material. I'm not unusual or special in any way. Besides, it's not in my nature to crave lots of new clothes and jewellery. At the end of the day whatever small pleasure they give you is only ephemeral. Too many possessions—whether clothes, jewellery or anything else—just make a person dissatisfied, because whatever they have it's never enough, and they always end up wanting more.'

Linking his long fingers together, Marco leant across the desk towards her, close enough that the scent of his arresting spicy cologne made her insides knot. 'If you agree to spend your holiday with me, what if buying you nice things makes *me* feel good?' he asked, his rich voice pitched intimately low.

She frowned. 'Marco…?'

'Yes, Grace?'

'You said you wanted a—a *companion* to join you on your break from work…'

'Specifically, a pleasant and attractive one…in *your* case a very beautiful one.'

Another woman would no doubt find such a lavish compliment coming from a man as extremely attractive and influential man as Marco a huge boost to her self-esteem…but not Grace. Ever since that frightening incident with her ex-boyfriend Chris she had deliberately steered clear of interested men. The truth was she was understandably nervous about giving them the wrong signals, and consequently about what they would expect if she inadvertently did so. There were times in the past when she might have been worryingly naive, but not any more. One of the most handsome and admired entrepreneurs in the world wouldn't ask a woman to be his companion for even a short time and not want something a bit more than her company she realised. *Hadn't he already alluded to similar arrangements with women?*

The shocking heat that suddenly suffused her at the idea made her nipples tingle and tighten beneath the flimsy silk of her camisole and she crossed her arms over her chest to prevent Marco from noting the fact. 'Is my company *all* that you want of me?' She blushed hard as she waited for his answer, in a state of tension in case he said, *No, that's not all that I want.*

Could she agree to his incredible offer to spend the rest of her holiday with him if it entailed something far more intimate and compromising than simply being a companion?

Resting his elbows on the desktop, Marco knew his hungry gaze was drinking her in like intoxicating wine—a wine that went immediately to his head. It simply wasn't possible for him to disguise the fact that he wanted her… If possible he wanted her even *more* after her assertion that she preferred the natural things in life—in particular the joy on the faces of children when an adult paid them some proper attention. Inwardly he had rejoiced with every fibre of his being when Grace had said that. Her words had acted like a salve on some of the desperate hurt he'd experienced as a child, and to be honest had knocked him sideways.

'You have asked me a straight question and I will give you a straight answer,' he replied. 'Yes I *do* want something other than your company. You are very different from most of the women I come into contact with, and that has an irresistible appeal for me. If, in the course of our time together, it should transpire that you share a similar fascination for me, then *yes*...of course I want to take you to bed.'

He shrugged a shoulder, as if it was a foregone conclusion. Her cheeks flushed as prettily as a wild rose in response, making his heart pound at even the mere idea of her slim but curvaceous body entwined with his in an embrace, let alone sharing the eroticism of lovemaking. It jolted him when Grace scraped back her chair and stood up.

'And is my receiving this cheque for the charity conditional on whether I accept your offer or not?'

Marco shook his head. Even if making his offer conditional *was* the only way to get her to sleep with him, he wouldn't do it. He might have a propensity sometimes to be a little ruthless in his business dealings, but he wouldn't be able to live with himself if he even attempted to coerce or blackmail a woman like Grace. She might be a self-confessed romantic but he didn't want to be the one to shatter that pretty illusion...

'No it isn't. The cheque is yours, come what may. You have my word on that.'

She sighed and her relief was palpable. 'Thank you. While we're talking so frankly, there's something I need to tell you. The thing is—the thing is sex isn't a simple or casual thing for me...I think you should know that.

Being a friend or companion to you while you're on a break is one thing…intimacy is entirely another.'

Saying nothing, Marco simply watched the visible interplay of emotions crossing her face, silently drawing his own conclusions about them.

'Can I give you my answer about this tomorrow?' she asked. 'Only I'd like some time to think it over. Also, in spite of my nap on your very comfortable couch, I'm still feeling rather tired. Do you mind if I don't stay for dinner? I hope your housekeeper hasn't gone to too much trouble getting the food ready…'

On his feet in a flash, Marco dropped his hands to his hips and ruefully shook his head. At least she hadn't given him a flat-out no in response to his frank admission that he wanted to take her to bed, he mused. As once again he fell under the spell of her incandescent crystal gaze he determinedly held onto that. Not that it had really surprised him when Grace told him that sex wasn't a simple or casual thing for her. Even before she'd revealed that nugget of information he'd sensed that she was a woman who would need to be seduced in the most subtle and artful of ways… If he was too demanding too soon she would quickly depart for good, never to be seen by him again, most likely. And now that he was set on making her his lover that was the very *last* scenario he wanted.

'Inês will be happy to accede to whatever arrangements I make for dinner—no matter how many times I may change them. What is much more important to me right now is that I have your promise that you *will* return tomorrow, Grace.'

'You have it. I'm a woman of my word, so I'll come back tomorrow and give you my answer then.'

'Good. If you follow me, we will go and find Miguel

to drive you home. In the morning he will return to your villa to collect you.'

'Thanks. Thanks also for taking me to lunch today. I really enjoyed the food *and* your company.' She smiled shyly, but then her glance darted helplessly to the cheque still lying on the desk.

Immediately Marco picked it up and handed it to her. 'You might want to post this to the charity.' He smiled, 'You can tell them that I will write soon, to confirm that I am in full agreement with them using it to help the children.'

'I'll also give them your address here, so that they can forward their thanks to you. Can you tell me what it is?'

He collected a sheet of personally addressed notepaper from the wooden letter-holder on his desk and gave it to her. Something told him she would put the task top of her list of priorities and the idea touching him, a warm sensation flooded into his heart.

'Well, I expect I should get home now.'

The shy smile that he was fast becoming addicted to returned.

'Let's go and find Miguel. I see now that you are indeed very tired. The sooner you get back to your villa and go to bed, the better.'

The repetitive thump on the villa's front door made Grace blearily open her eyes. Turning her head, she glanced at the clock sitting atop the neat pine cabinet and released a disbelieving groan followed by a very unladylike curse. Good God! She'd slept the evening and the night away. She hadn't stirred once, not even to go to the loo. Now it was a little after ten, and some determined caller sounded as if they were intent on breaking down her door. Her dad wouldn't be best pleased if they caused any damage…

Even as she had the thought she remembered that Marco had promised to send his car for her, to take her back to the palatial mansion that was his residence. Then she remembered the *reason* for her return. Her insides did a one-hundred-and-eighty degree roll. She muttered another ripe curse. *How could she have forgotten such a commitment for even a second?* No matter *how* tired she was?

Grabbing the short textured cotton robe at the end of the bed, she hurriedly got to her feet and pulled it on over her matching white nightdress. Barefoot, she flung open the door and moved quickly down the cool tiled corridor that led to the front of the house.

'*Olà,* Senhorita Faulkner.'

The chauffeur Miguel stood on the other side of the door. Conscious that her hair was tousled and uncombed, and that her short robe perhaps revealed too much leg for her to be comfortable displaying in front of almost a stranger, Grace pulled the sides of the garment more securely round her, then lightly knotted the belt. 'Hello, Miguel,' she answered, silently noting the faint surprise in his deep black eyes that she had addressed him by his name. 'I'm really sorry but I'm afraid I overslept. As you can see, I've just got out of bed, and I'm nowhere near ready to leave yet. Do you want to come back for me later…after lunch, maybe?'

'No, Senhorita Faulkner. Senhor Aguilar will not be happy if I do not return with you this morning, as arranged.'

She could well believe it. A man who probably just had to snap his fingers to have his every whim fulfilled would clearly *not* be happy if Grace had the audacity to be late…especially when he had been so generous with his donation to the charity. She didn't know much about the culture in Portugal, but she'd heard via her dad that to be late for an appointment with someone—especially someone high up the business world hierarchy—was considered a serious lack of respect.

'In that case you'll just have to come in and wait while I get myself ready.' She held the door wide to allow the chauffeur entrance into the hallway, but he stayed right where he was, his tanned face impassive as a rock.

'I am sorry, Senhorita Faulkner, but that would not be at all appropriate. In any case I must phone Senhor Aguilar right away and explain the reason for our delay. Then I will wait for you in the car.'

Grace watched him walk with purposeful gait back to the gleaming black Mercedes parked outside the villa's entrance, with its climbing red and pink bougainvillaea trailing up traditional white-painted walls. Then she turned on her heel and headed straight for the bathroom and the quickest shower she could manage—all the while apprehensively contemplating what her answer should be when Marco Aguilar asked her if she'd decided whether or not she would become his companion for the rest of her time in the Algarve.

Remembering the cheque he'd donated to the charity, and imagining what joy such an amount would bring to everyone concerned with the desperate and poor orphaned children it had been set up to help support, she already knew that his offer would be hard to turn down. Yesterday, when she'd sensed that Marco had very definitely *not* come to terms with his emotionally impoverished childhood it had made her want to know more about this darkly enigmatic man. And when she thought about the way he made her feel, the effect he had on her body... Maybe if she allowed herself to experience intimacy with him it might be a way to help herself overcome the pain of her ex's attempted rape and allow her to move on psychologically too, and truly put that horrific episode behind her?

On her arrival at the palatial villa, his housekeeper Inês greeted her with the invitation to wait in garden while Marco finished an important phone call. Sitting under a parasol in her host's incredibly beautiful private shaded garden, Grace made herself breathe out very slowly to help calm her nerves. Her time with Marco yesterday had taken on the surreal quality of an unbelievable dream. Finding herself yet again with the prospect of not only his arresting company but a conversation she was bound by promise to have with him about his proposition it was surely understandable that she should be seized by sudden nerves?

Reaching for the long cool glass of lemonade that Inês had thoughtfully brought her, she glanced down at the sleeveless red and white maxi-dress that she'd donned. It was one of only two dresses she had packed to come out here, and it was pretty and cool in the heat and indisputably feminine. It certainly wasn't the kind of clothing she wore every day. At work she invariably got away with the much more casual attire of T-shirt and jeans, and sometimes a trouser suit if she had to go a meeting with a potential patron. Now she was glad of the protection of the parasol, as already she sensed her exposed shoulders were frying a little beneath the hot sun.

She sipped her drink. Time ticked by. A drowsy buzzing insect flew right by her ear and startled her. She wondered how long Marco would be, then decided there was no option other than to try and relax and simply enjoy a garden that had all the seductive attributes of a floral sensual paradise. Sighing, she briefly shut her eyes to appreciate more fully the sweet bouquet of the yellow and white gardenias that wafted beneath her nose and the hypnotic sound of the splashing waterfall just a few feet from where she sat.

But suddenly impinging on her enjoyment came the contrasting images and sounds of an African city slum, where the poorly erected houses were fashioned from mud and metal and where the children played in an area teeming with heaving mounds of garbage. *The heat there was unbearable and stifling, and made even more intense by the ever-present heavy smog...*

The disturbing memory jolted her sickeningly and tears of compassion and frustration because more people didn't try and do something to alleviate the situation surged hotly into her eyes.

'My sincere apologies for keeping you waiting, Grace. Ah... I see that Inês has given you a cool drink? That's good. Today is going to be even hotter than yesterday, I believe.'

She hadn't heard his soft-footed approach across the grass, and when she opened her eyes to acknowledge the figure that instantly captivated her gaze, the nerves she'd tried hard to subdue sprang into unsettling life again. The sight of Marco wearing an immaculate white shirt, with the sleeves casually rolled up to just beneath his elbows, and fawn-coloured chinos that were clearly meant to be equally casual but on his tall, athletic frame looked effortlessly stylish and elegant too made her heartbeat hop, skip and jump, and her mouth turned as dry as though she hadn't had a drop of water to drink for days.

Before she could summon up words of greeting, he moved towards her and leaned down to plant a sizzling little kiss at the corner of her startled lips.

'I—I didn't mind waiting,' she responded at last, with

the imprint of his warm mouth lingering disturbingly, like an intimate brand. 'It's so lovely out here, and anyway…it was *me* that was late in the first place. I'm sorry about that, by the way. I overslept.'

'So Miguel explained.' His dark eyes twinkled. Then he pulled out the sunchair opposite Grace at the table and adjusted the aviator sunglasses he'd been wearing on the top of his head over his eyes.

Now it would be impossible for her to guess what he was thinking…

His unexpectedly personal greeting had set off a veritable firework display of reaction inside her, and she knew that any remaining reservations she had about accepting his offer were assuredly being demolished one by one.

She made a discreet attempt to wipe the moisture from her eyes that had arisen when she'd mentally been transported back to Africa and her handsome companion frowned. 'Is everything all right? You seem a little upset,' he commented.

'I'm fine.' She made herself respond with a reassuring smile, even though the slight quaver in her voice no doubt made a liar of her.

'I do not entirely believe you, but I hope you can put whatever troubles you to one side so that you can enjoy the day. It is far too beautiful to be sad, yes?'

Marco wondered at the cause of the distress reflected in Grace's crystal-clear blue eyes. *He prayed it wasn't bad news from home that would make her cut short her stay.* He schooled himself to relax, studying her pleasingly curvaceous form in the very becoming red and white dress, her golden hair curling prettily down over her shoulders. The arresting sigh of her intensified the drugging sensual heat that had already invaded him at the prospect of seeing her again.

Anticipating the long break that he intended, he'd informed all of this morning's telephone callers that he would only be contactable if there was an emergency— at the back of his mind had been the irresistible thought that he intended to be far too preoccupied with the lovely girl he'd found himself infatuated with to think about business. The kiss he'd planted at the corner of Grace's pretty mouth just now had been an exciting revelation. Her skin was softer than velvet and down combined. *She'd smelled irresistible too.* Recognising the alluring French scent, he made a mental note to send some to her villa as a gift.

Now he would not wait a moment longer to ask her the question that had ensured he'd more or less had a sleepless night because he hadn't been able to stop dwelling upon the outcome of it...

'So, Grace... I trust you have now had plenty of time to think over my proposition? What will be your answer, I wonder?'

CHAPTER FIVE

GRACE didn't answer him straight away, but appeared to be thinking deeply. He knew it was in his nature to be impatient, but the tension that gathered in the pit of Marco's stomach as he waited for her to speak made him feel as if he was wearing an increasingly tightening iron band round his middle. No woman had ever said no to spending time with him before...was this engaging British girl going to be the *first*?

Folding her hands in her lap, she locked her brilliant blue gaze with his at last and a tentative smile gently raised the corners of her lips. 'My answer is... Well, it's *yes*. And I'm going to be honest with you... The reason I've said yes is that I—I...' Gnawing at her lip her cheeks turned engagingly pink.

'Go on,' Marco encouraged.

'I've discovered that I *am* attracted to you. Otherwise I wouldn't consider it—no matter how lovely the inducements. And I was going to be on my own the entire time I was here, and now I have someone to share my holiday with...I'm grateful.'

He'd told her once before that her honesty was refreshing, but never had it mattered more to him than right now. She knew exactly what he was asking and had accepted the offer he'd made because she was attracted to him.

She hadn't run away or taken refuge behind being coy.
She had admitted that she liked him outright. Now there
was no need for any tedious mind games or manipula-
tion. All they had to do was let nature take its course.
Marco had not the slightest doubt that it would...

'I'm very pleased you've accepted my offer, Grace.
Now all we have to do is get to know each other a little and enjoy ourselves.' Rising to his feet, he took her
by the hands and gently urged her up from her chair.
'Fortunately you are perfectly dressed for what I have
in mind today. Some time ago I received an invitation
from a business acquaintance of mine to attend a garden
party she is having. At the time I told her I wasn't sure
whether I would even be in the country, but now that I
am and you have agreed to be my companion...I think
we will go.'

'A garden party, you say?'

Still holding onto her hands, and noticing the brief
flare of doubt in her eyes, Marco smiled. 'You know...?
Champagne, exquisite food, music played soothingly in
the background by a specially hired professional ensemble and some amicable conversation with our host and
the other guests in a setting just as beautiful as this...
It's the perfect way to start our holiday together, don't
you agree?'

'It all sounds rather grand. The garden parties I've personally experienced have been on a much more modest
scale...usually thrown by my mum and dad. My mum
spends the entire week before frantically cleaning the
house and planning what food to buy, while my dad is
relegated to the garden to cut the grass and make sure
the barbecue is clean and ready for use. The guests are
generally extended family and friends—some of whom
have young children. There's no soothing music play-

ing, but generally there's plenty of hilarity and laughter amongst the children playing on my dad's pristine newly cut lawn.' Grimacing, she gently tugged her captive hands free to smooth them down over her dress, 'I'm sorry… I'm babbling again. That's because I'm nervous.'

'Am I so intimidating that you have to be nervous of me?' Marco frowned, quite charmed by her sharing of the experience of garden parties with her parents and their friends. Silently he attested to feeling rather envious of Grace's very normal-sounding and happy family life. In contrast to growing up without parents or any other family at all how could he *not*? 'Now that you have accepted my invitation, I'd like to think you can relax and just be yourself around me. If you are wary of me for any reason then you will put up a guard, and that is the very last thing I want.'

'I've never met anyone like you before, Marco.' He heard the quiet intake of breath she softly released. 'And I've certainly never been around great wealth or fame before. I'll try not to be intimidated by you, or the company you keep, but I can't pretend it won't be a challenge. I'm a girl from a very ordinary background, and I've never mixed with the kind of people who inhabit your world. I still can't understand why you'd even ask someone like me to spend time with you. Surely you must…you must know plenty of much more suitable women?'

'If you knew these so-called "more suitable" women, you would not even ask me that question, Grace.'

Folding his arms across his chest, Marco realised he was feeling quite bereft because she'd withdrawn her hands from his clasp. He yearned to grab them back and hold them again. Already he was addicted to the touch of her peerlessly soft skin.

'Now I have to go and locate my bodyguard José. I

regret we have to attend this function with a third party accompanying us, I really do. But I know for a fact that the paparazzi will be very much in evidence this afternoon, and they can be intimidating—even to those of us who are quite familiar with the lengths they will go to in order to get a picture. Sit down, relax and enjoy the sunshine. I will be back soon.'

There...she'd done it. She'd said yes to Marco Aguilar's astonishing invitation to spend the remainder of her holiday with him in the full knowledge that she was also agreeing to a short affair.

Just the thought made her feel weak. But it wasn't the kind of weakness that emanated from being frightened, she realized. Quite the *opposite*, in fact. A frisson of shivering excitement ran through her. She was twenty-five and had not yet experienced having a lover. Because of her highly upsetting and demoralising experience she had kept men at a distance—but the truth was she had often yearned to know what it would be like to have someone make love to her that really liked and regarded her. Ultimately she yearned for a man to love her with all his heart, but if she refused to give in to her fears of being hurt again being with Marco might turn out to be an important step on the road to healing the shadows that dogged her. Fervently, Grace hoped so.

Sighing, she mentally shook her head in wonder at the extraordinary situation she found herself in. Now that she'd committed herself to going through with Marco's request to be his companion she was determined to try and be more confident and face everything. That included every potentially intimidating situation she might encounter during the next few days—situations that would no doubt occur simply because she was in this man's revered company.

To help her deal with whatever challenges might arise she would simply remind herself that when her totally unexpected sojourn with him was at an end she would return home to London, to her normal everyday routine and her work with the children's charity. The upside of that was that she would be returning with the knowledge that—thanks to Marco—the charity now had the necessary funds to rebuild the orphanage. It would make a monumental difference to the orphaned and abandoned children she'd so come to love, and that made everything else pale into insignificance.

She dropped back down into the comfortable sunchair, and into her mind stole the memory of Marco's voice saying, 'If, in the course of our time together, it should transpire that you share a similar fascination for me, then, yes…of course I want to take you to bed.' *Well, she she'd admitted that she was attracted to him. Now all she had to do was just let things unfold and see what happened.* It sounded so easy, but Grace knew it was anything *but*…

Arranging her sunglasses back in front of her eyes, she found her avid glance cleaving to the arresting sight of his tall, athletic figure strolling nonchalantly back across the verdant grass to the house…

As he pointed out various interesting landmarks on the hour long drive to his friend's residence, Marco's level tone definitely conveyed pride. Yet Grace detected a strange *ambivalence* too. As if he was somehow conflicted about his right to take pleasure in his beautiful country. She couldn't help but be intrigued by the thought. But then, the more time she spent in his striking presence, the more she became intrigued by everything about him. Sometimes when he leaned nearer to her, to point out something of interest through the passenger window, she breathed in the subtly arousing warmth of his body that mingled with his expensive spicy cologne and everything in her tightened and contracted, in case she completely yielded to the disturbingly powerful urge to touch him that so worryingly kept enveloping her.

'We are here.'

Miguel, with the much bigger-built José in the passenger seat next to him, drove the sleek Mercedes up to the tall iron gates that had appeared at the end of a narrow road shaded with tall pines. Just before they reached those imposing barriers Grace saw several cars haphazardly parked in front of them, and their waiting owners hurriedly exiting their vehicles with high-tech cameras in tow. She sucked in a breath. At the same time she sensed Marco's cool hand firmly slide over hers.

'There is nothing to worry about, *meu querida*. They will get their pictures and then hopefully leave us alone. If not, José will help them to do just that.'

There was a distinct twinkle in his deep brown eyes as his glance met hers, and her stomach plummeted again— but this time with pleasure.

As soon as the car manoeuvred to a stop in front of the gates the photographers literally swarmed over it, their fast-flashing cameras and camcorders all trained on Marco and Grace seated in the back. José had climbed out as the vehicle had glided to a halt, and Grace heard him shout commandingly at the voracious throng to clear a space so that they could drive through the gates. She heard plenty of curses and yelps of protest too, as he physically removed bodies from climbing across the car's bonnet, with intrusive cameras pointing at the windscreen in a bid to get pictures of Marco and his guest.

With her heart pounding, Grace turned to glance out through the tinted window beside her at the exact same moment as a camera flash blinded her from seeing anything other than that disorientating bright light.

José jumped back into the front seat and shouted, 'Go!' as a uniformed man standing behind the gates spoke urgently into a mobile, nodded towards the car in recognition of its VIP passenger, and stood aside as the now opening electronic gates allowed the vehicle entry.

As the gates rapidly closed again behind them, Marco tapped on the small front window separating him and Grace from the two men in the front. When the window immediately opened, he leaned forward to speak to his bodyguard. Although she didn't understand what he said, because he spoke in his native Portuguese, Grace intuited by the concern in his voice that he was asking his employee if he was okay. The intrepid José must have taken quite a few knocks dealing with the unruly mob that had accosted their car, she realised.

The window closed again and Marco leaned back in the luxuriously upholstered leather seat, cursing softly beneath his breath.

'Is José all right?' she ventured.

'He's fine. He has dealt with much worse than that before, I assure you. Now, let us forget about that rabble at the gates and try to enjoy ourselves…okay?'

After driving for a while through stunningly landscaped gardens, with orange, lemon and tall palm trees lining the straight drive that led to the dazzling white villa that was their destination, Marco's chauffeur steered the car onto a sickle-shaped gravelled area that was already filled with impressively gleaming vehicles. Grace's stomach plunged at the prospect of meeting and mingling with other no doubt extremely wealthy and important people like Marco. In a moment of doubt and uncertainty her fingers curled anxiously into the crisp cotton of her dress. She sent up a silent heartfelt plea for help.

Miguel politely helped her out of the car. As she straightened she briefly met his eyes and saw that they had a reassuring twinkle in them, as if he'd intuited how overwhelmed she must be feeling and wanted to lend his support. José was already standing outside, conversing quietly with Marco. As she tentatively moved towards the man who was his boss, Marco caught hold of her hand and smiled.

'Grace...this is the home of—'

'Marco!'

The loud male shout made them both turn round abruptly. Hurrying towards them was a well-built middle-aged man in a smart petrol-blue suit and an open-necked white silk shirt, with the kind of craggy good-looks that suggested the legacy of a life well lived and perhaps a little *too* over-indulgent?

A ripple of surprised recognition went through Grace. *Lincoln Roberts*...The man was a seriously famous movie-star, whose visit to rehab in California a couple of years ago had been splashed all over the tabloid newspapers...as had his previous affair with another star's very young wife. Was that why Marco had known for a fact that the paparazzi would be very much in evidence this afternoon? An A-list celebrity like Lincoln was bound to attract major interest.

'So glad you could make it, my friend. Francesca and I were afraid you wouldn't. God knows, you're a hard man to pin down!' The well-known actor gave the businessman a brief hug and then, before releasing him, slapped him affectionately on the back.

'I was pleased to be invited. You're looking well, Lincoln. Very well.'

Marco sounded somewhat reserved, despite his words, and the edges of his well-cut lips lifted in a smile that was quite some way short of being as open as his friend's. When he stepped back and automatically reached for Grace's hand, to enfold it almost possessively inside his palm, a distinct wave of warmth and pleasure quivered through her.

'Thanks. I've been taking much better care of myself since I've been with Francesca. The woman has transformed me! By the way, she'll be along any moment now. She's powdering her nose…you know what women are like! And who's *this* lovely lady that you've brought with you?' Lincoln asked, his interested, almost *greedy* blue eyed glance moving from Grace's face down to the modest cleavage of her dress in one disturbing swoop.

She found herself moving a little closer to Marco's side, as if subconsciously seeking his protection. Lincoln Roberts might be one of the most famous movie stars on the planet, but she knew almost instantly that she didn't like him…didn't like him *one bit*.

'This is Grace Faulkner.'

Marco had provided the other man with her name almost reluctantly, Grace thought.

'A beautiful name for an undoubtedly beautiful lady… I'm delighted to make your acquaintance, Grace. I really am.'

In a blink he had separated her hand from Marco's and clasped it firmly between his own bigger, slightly *sweaty* palms. It was hard not to cringe. 'It's nice to meet you too, Mr Roberts,' she murmured politely, at the same time quickly disengaging her hand.

'Call me Lincoln, sweetheart. We don't stand on ceremony here. Francesca wants all her guests to feel relaxed and to make themselves at home. These little gatherings she has are always very informal...aren't they, Marco?'

'They are indeed.'

'Talk of the devil—here she is now. Doesn't she look ravishing?'

'*Ciao*, Marco...I'm so glad that you were able to come. I doubted that you would, you know...'

Both men turned to greet the vision in figure-hugging white that had joined them. The dark-eyed brunette with her perfectly arched eyebrows and scarlet-painted lips had straight away made a beeline for Marco and was regarding him with undisguised pleasure, Grace noticed, watching apprehensively as the woman kissed him resoundingly on both cheeks, then dropped slender hands with myriad glinting diamond rings lightly yet almost *possessively* onto his arms.

'Handsome as ever, I see. Broken any poor woman's heart lately—like you broke mine?'

Grace's stomach flipped as she waited to hear his answer.

'No. And I doubt very much that *any* man could break *your* heart, Francesca.'

Their eyes locked for a scant second, and Grace didn't think she imagined the regret in the Italian woman's beautiful dark gaze. *Did Marco feel the same?* She was about to distance herself from him a little when he turned towards her, smiled, then once again, enfolded her hand in his.

'Grace, this is Francesca Bellini, our charming hostess. She is becoming a force to be reckoned with in the world of high fashion. Francesca, I'd like to introduce Grace Faulkner.'

'Grace...delighted to meet you.' The woman shook her hand limply and almost instantly let it go. She was anything *but* delighted, Grace thought wryly. Clearly she and Marco had once been an item, and it was obvious that the Italian wished that they still *were*. The realisation didn't exactly bode well for a relaxed afternoon...

Lincoln stepped in just then, to loop his arm round his girlfriend's tiny waist, cinched in with a broad patent leather white belt with a huge gold buckle. Could she even *breathe* in such a tight outfit? Grace wondered. She was suddenly very glad of her own more comfortable and practical summer dress.

'Darling, I was just telling Grace that our parties here are always very relaxed, informal affairs.' The American smiled.

Informal and *relaxed* weren't the two descriptions that naturally sprang to mind, Grace wryly reflected as she scanned the perfectly manicured grass that ran down to a shimmering blue lake with two pairs of regal swans gliding across it, then looked back again to the sight of small clusters of guests dressed glamorously enough for a garden party at Buckingham Palace.

To add to the indisputable impression of the kind of wealth that went far beyond most ordinary people's dreams, on the air floated the sound of a well-known Vivaldi composition played by a sublime string quartet. Grace immediately had the strongest urge to move closer to where the musicians were performing, so that she could simply stand in the sunshine and listen to them play at close quarters. It would be such a privilege, she thought.

She glanced up at the dark-eyed man by her side, and something told her that *he* too would infinitely prefer to do just that, rather than spend too much time with their hostess and her infamous boyfriend.

The knowledge made her suddenly bold, and briefly

buried her disquiet that Marco should bring her to a garden party at the house of an ex-girlfriend. 'Is that lovely music being played nearby?' she asked, proffering what she hoped was an eager and appreciative but not too *presumptuous* smile to the party's glamorous hosts.

'Yes, honey—they're sitting right over there by the fountain,' Lincoln answered.

'It sounds so wonderful. Marco? Shall we go over and see them?'

'Go ahead,' Francesca urged helpfully, but not before Grace had witnessed the undisguised flash of jealousy in her glance. 'I'm sure we'll hook up again later. By the way, there are a lot of people you know here already, plus a few that you *don't* who are anxious to meet you. In the meantime, go and enjoy the music with the beautiful Grace.'

When they were less than halfway across the shimmering lawn that led to a spectacular fountain with an audacious sculpted mermaid, Grace murmured, 'I hope you didn't mind that I suggested going to listen to the quartet?'

Touching his hand to her bare arm, Marco came to a standstill. Staring back at him in surprise, she saw the frown that creased his tanned brow as his dark eyes thoughtfully roved her face. 'Francesca and I dated for a short while about five years ago. These days she is no more than a business acquaintance I occasionally bump into at corporate functions. Did you think that she meant something more to me than that? As far as I know she is quite happy to have her name linked with a movie star like Lincoln. She's always been very ambitious, and their romantic partnership certainly hasn't hurt her career.'

'She's seriously stunning.'

'So?'

'I just wondered why you would bring me to a party thrown by an ex-girlfriend. I know we're not serious or anything, but—'

'I told you…we were over a long time ago and there's nothing for you to worry about. Can't we simply enjoy the party?'

Grace shrugged, feeling slightly miserable that she might be spoiling things between them before they'd really even begun. 'Okay.'

'Come here.'

'What?'

'I said come here.'

Catching hold of her by her slim upper arms, Marco impelled her against him so that she was suddenly on dizzyingly intimate terms with the hard, lean physique she'd been secretly admiring since setting eyes on him again that morning. The heat from his body all but burned her through the elegant cotton of his shirt.

Tipping up her face, he gazed down at her, saying, 'You know…I have a sudden profound urge to make you stop talking.'

The unexpected confession was accompanied by the most enigmatic of heart-stopping smiles. His seductive warm lips covered hers. She didn't even have time to gasp her surprise.

It was a kiss that sent a molten river of irresistible longing pumping right through her body, and Grace's lips parted almost the instant he touched his lips to hers. Less than a moment later her knees all but threatened to fold at the hotly melting exploration of his erotically silken tongue. Her hands automatically moved either side of his straight lean hips to anchor herself.

Just when the incredible assault on her senses felt as if it might grow even stronger—turn into a veritable wildfire that would burn them both to cinders with its power—Marco cupped the side of her face with a warm palm and gently and regretfully separated his mouth from hers. 'I desired to stop you talking so that I could sample the sweetness of your lips…but now I am almost rendered speechless myself due to the fire you have stoked in me, Grace.'

He meant every word.

Inside his chest, Marco's heart was thundering in an amalgam of desire, urgent longing and deep, deep shock at the depth of feeling that kissing this woman had aroused in him. All he could think right then was that he wished he hadn't been so hasty in making the decision to come to Francesca Bellini's garden party—if he were at home now with Grace he would be making it his mission to get her into bed…

Carefully moving her to his side, Marco slipped a deceptively casual arm round her waist, just so that he could maintain the contact that was becoming the most essential factor of all for determining his happiness that day—especially after that explosive little kiss they'd just shared. He was still walking on air from the sheer pleasure of it.

'Let's go and listen to the music together, shall we? I've heard this particular string quartet perform before at La Scala in Milan…'

After some companionable time had passed, during which Grace and Marco sat side by side sipping champagne on the edge of the sculpted fountain, listening to the sublime soaring notes of Vivaldi's *Four Seasons*, Marco was invited to join the well-dressed group of businessmen and women who had been eyeing him ever since he'd walked across the perfect emerald lawn to sit by the water fountain with Grace.

Assuring him that she was quite happy to sit there by herself for a while as he conversed with them, Grace shut her eyes to simply let the stirring music envelop her. It had the same delicious effect as cooling summer rain after a hot, dry spell. In truth, she was glad of the opportunity not just to listen to the music but to mull silently over the soul-stirring kiss that Marco had initiated and she had eagerly complied with.

It had been a revelation just how much she'd enjoyed it. Since that dreadful incident with her ex-boyfriend she'd secretly feared another man kissing her, in case she was immediately repelled by the contact. But the *opposite* had happened. Even now the memory of Marco's lips against hers made her tingle fiercely and long for more… *much* more of the same. She briefly held her breath at the thought, then batted away a buzzing insect that brushed against her cheek. The day was once again incredibly hot, and the soporific intensity of it was making her drowsy. She wished that she'd remembered to bring the straw hat she'd left lying on a chair in her villa's hallway.

Just then there was a break in the music, and when Grace opened her eyes she was taken aback to find a small auburn-haired girl standing in front her. The child's skin was as fair as her own, but she was sensibly wearing a sunhat, its brim decorated with very becoming pink and white daisies.

'What's *your* name?' the girl demanded, head tipped to one side and jade-green eyes squinting in the sunshine.

Grace smiled. 'My name is Grace,' she answered. 'What's yours?'

'I'm Cindy Mae Roberts and I'm here with my daddy. He's a movie star.'

Glancing round the various little knots of men and women gathered together on the rolling lawn, Grace saw this little girl appeared to be the only child there. Instantly Grace's heart went out to her, perhaps doubly so because she had the onerous legacy of Lincoln Roberts' world-wide fame to contend with growing up. 'Well, Cindy, I'm very pleased to meet you.'

She held out her hand but the child ignored it, demanding instead, 'Are you in the movies? If you are I've never heard of you.'

'That's because I'm not…in the movies, I mean.'

'Then what *do* you do?'

'I work in London for a charity that helps children who are orphaned and abandoned.'

'That must be *so* boring!'

Grace's lips curved in a gently understanding smile. 'It's not boring at all…it's quite the opposite, in fact. It's wonderful to help make children happy—especially children who don't have any parents or anyone else to love them and look after them. It's very satisfying.'

An expression crossed Cindy's freckled face that was surprisingly thoughtful. 'Do you really like children, then?'

'Of course. I like them very much.'

'My daddy doesn't. He just thinks they're a nuisance… At least, he thinks *I* am. I'm glad I only stay with him now and again, because sometimes he's not very nice. The other times I live with my mom in New York…she's *very* nice.'

Now Grace's heart really *did* go out to the girl. What a horrible thing for any child to believe…that her father thought her a nuisance. She noticed that Cindy held a lime-green tennis ball down by her side. 'Didn't any other children come to the garden party for you to play with?' she asked.

'No. My daddy said one little nuisance was enough, without inviting any more, and Francesca agreed. She doesn't like children either.'

Grimacing at that, Grace immediately got to her feet. 'How about a game of catch?' she suggested, smoothing her hands down over her dress and at the same time kicking off her backless sandals, then bending down to pick them up and carry them.

The child's vivid green eyes lit up like a light bulb. 'Really? I'd love that!'

'Good. Then let's go and find a big patch of grass where we won't get in the way of people with their drinks.'

'Sure.' The child unhesitatingly slipped her hand trustingly in Grace's and beamed up at her with a look of unconstrained anticipation and delight.

CHAPTER SIX

Marco was looking for Grace, but she'd somehow disappeared. He'd met and conversed with a few people from the corporate world with genuinely interesting ideas and a couple of business propositions they'd asked him to think about, but none of them—neither the people nor the ideas—held his attention like *she* did. Now he experienced a sense of irritation mingled with discomfiting panic that he couldn't find her. *Where had she got to, for goodness' sake?* Had it been too much to ask for her to wait for him by the fountain where he'd left her?

After asking a couple of guests nearby if they'd seen a very attractive blonde wearing a long red and white dress, and having them regretfully shake their heads, a frustrated Marco headed across the grass to where his two loyal employees were deep in conversation by the parked cars.

'Have either of you seen Miss Faulkner?' he demanded.

'She's over there by the pine trees.' Miguel pointed helpfully, with what appeared to be an almost indulgent and knowing smile crossing his face. 'She's playing catch with Senhor Roberts' young daughter. There are no other children here, and she said that the child was looking for somebody to play with her.'

'So naturally Miss Faulkner volunteered?' Feeling somewhat bemused, Marco thought wryly that he shouldn't be surprised. It seemed that whenever children's needs were on the radar Grace would somehow be involved. He'd had no idea that Lincoln even *had* a daughter, because the man had never so much as mentioned her in his hearing. Clearly that didn't bode well for her. *Poor kid...*

He found himself reflecting that there wasn't one other single woman he knew who would put a child's enjoyment before her own, or potentially give up the chance to make an impression—especially at a gathering like this, where celebrities and influential guests could literally be picked off like cherries from a tree...

'She has a very kind heart,' his chauffeur observed— *unnecessarily*, Marco thought.

'Her conduct so far definitely seems to bear that out,' he commented. 'In any case, I think I will go and join her. The pair of you should go and get yourselves a drink. It is a particularly hot day, no?'

'Yes, boss.'

'And stop grinning like I'm the butt of some kind of joke I don't know about!'

'Yes, boss.'

Shrugging irritably, Marco turned away to stride down towards the bank of pine trees, where he'd already caught a glimpse of Grace's very fetching red and white dress and the bright banner of a child's auburn hair.

His elusive lady had missed her catch and dropped down onto one knee, laughing out loud as the small girl standing a few feet away from her clapped her hands together and squealed in delight, 'I caught you out again! I thought you'd get better but you're really not very good at this at all, are you?' she taunted.

'That's why they called me butter-fingers at school,' Grace replied good-humouredly. And then in the next instant her cornflower-blue eyes widened when she saw that Marco stood watching them. Now *he* was the lucky recipient of her bright, engaging smile. 'Hi, there,' she called out, 'did you have a good time chatting with your friends?'

He had the same incredulous reaction he probably would have had if he'd been singled out for special attention by the Queen of England herself. Warring with a great desire to grin back at her like some infatuated schoolboy, instead he shaped his lips into a sardonically tinged smile. 'I was not "chatting with my friends" as you so ingenuously put it, Grace. You do not "chat" with a prominent executive of the Banco de Portugal as if he were a long-lost buddy you last saw in the school playground!'

'Obviously not, if he takes himself as seriously as *you* do.'

Dumbstruck by her audacity, Marco nonetheless saw the funny side of Grace's lightning-quick irreverent reply. Before the idea had even formed in his mind he was striding across the perfectly mown grass to take hold of her by the waist and haul her to her feet. 'You deserve to be severely punished for that,' he told her, a husky catch in his voice.

The laughter in her eyes immediately died. It was replaced by the kind of fearful look that shocked Marco to his boots. She was genuinely terrified, he saw. He instantly released her. Inside his chest his heart was thumping as hard as a blacksmith's hammer striking an anvil.

'I was only joking,' he stared back into her apprehensive glance ruefully shaking his head. 'Are you okay? Do you always react like this when a man makes a harmless jest?'

'No.' She forced a smile, but distinct wariness had replaced the joyful laughter of only a few moments ago.

Marco felt as if he'd just lost something precious.

'You took me by surprise, that's all,' she finished.

Her soft golden hair had been tousled by her energetic game with the girl and lay across her pale satin shoulders in inviting buttery curls. God help him, but he ached to drive his fingers through those silken strands and then lift them away from her beautiful face so that he could kiss her passionately —just as he'd dared to do earlier, when they'd been heading towards the fountain to listen to the music. Only this time he would not be in any hurry to relinquish those petal-soft lips for anyone or *anything.*

'I apologise if I frightened you. That was definitely *not* my intention. I came to find you to tell you that the buffet is ready and I think we should go and eat. Will you come with me?'

He despised the uncertainty he heard in his voice— uncertainty that Grace would agree to go *anywhere* with him after that look of dread on her face when he had hauled her to her feet to chastise her playfully. For a woman to have such a hold over him that she made him doubt his powers of persuasion, the fact that he could have anything he wanted and not be refused, was *dangerous*, he reflected. *A genuine first for him…*

To Marco's intense relief she nodded, shrugging the slender shoulders exposed by her sleeveless dress. 'Of course. I *am* feeling rather hungry come to think of it. Cindy can come with us. By the way, Cindy is Lincoln Roberts' daughter—perhaps you two have met before?'

'No. I have not had the privilege.' He turned to smile at the auburn-haired girl with the bright green eyes that she must have inherited from her mother. None of her dainty features remotely resembled her father's. She was moving warily towards them. When she was level he lightly shook her hand. 'I'm very pleased to meet you Cindy. My name is Marco.'

'Marco Aguilar?'

He frowned in amusement. The child had sounded much older than her years when she'd asked that. 'That's right.'

'My daddy told me to mind my manners if I spoke to you. He said that you're a very important man…very *rich* too.'

Forming a nonchalant smile, nonetheless Marco was irritated. The child's innocent remark had once again brought home the sobering fact that he only seemed to be of interest to people because of his wealth and suc-cess—*not* because they enjoyed his company. For years now he'd been okay with that. He was a realist like he'd told Grace. But lately, for some reason, his wealth and success didn't seem to be enough to fill the sense of emp-tiness inside him.

'Grace and I are going to get some lunch. Would you like to join us?' Deciding that it was probably best to ignore the child's comments—after all, she wasn't re-sponsible for her father's mercenary attitude—he chose to press on with his own plans.

'No, thanks. I'm going back to my room for a while. Thanks for playing catch with me, Grace…even though you can't catch! Will you be okay with Mr Aguilar?' The green eyes flashed suspiciously as they turned back to Marco.

He shrugged ironically as he glanced from her over to Grace. 'Think you'll be okay with me?' he asked lightly, praying he would never see that haunted look of fear in her eyes ever again.

'Of course I'll be okay,' she settled her gaze confidently on Cindy. 'Mr Aguilar is a friend…a friend that I *trust*,' she told her.

Warmth cascaded into his insides at her unhesitating reply.

'Bye, then.' With a brief wave, the small girl danced away.

'She acts a bit like a prickly pear, but underneath she's a sweet little thing,' Grace murmured, colouring a little as she bent down to the grass to slip her sandals back on. 'She just needs her father to show her a bit more love and affection—that's my guess.'

The observation made Marco feel a little hollow inside, because he knew that it was most likely true. 'You certainly looked as though you were enjoying yourselves.'

'It's always good to remind yourself what fun it can be to behave like a child again. It helps us grown-ups not to be so serious, don't you think?'

'I'm sure that's true—if you were lucky enough to experience having fun as a child. Not everyone is so fortunate.' The words were out before Marco had the chance to check them. Feeling awkward, and annoyed that he'd inadvertently revealed something about his past that he normally took pains to conceal, he felt hot, embarrassed colour sear his cheeks.

'Marco? I'm sorry if I—'

'Let's go and get some food, shall we? And you ought to get out of this heat for a while. You look hot and flushed after your exertions, Grace. We'll go and find some shade.'

Grace couldn't honestly have recounted what she'd eaten that day if anybody had asked. The food that had been laid out so abundantly and extravagantly onto the white linen cloths at the buffet tables had been a colourful and sumptuous banquet. Yet it hadn't tempted her at all. She'd merely picked at the few items that a waitresses had put on her plate.

After the comment Marco had made suggesting that not everyone was lucky enough to remember having fun as a child, she'd lapsed into a quiet reverie about him, her mind tumbling with questions that she ached to have answers to. He was a man that to the acquisitive outside world seemed to have everything anyone could ever want—certainly in terms of a successful career and the material wealth that it had brought him. But behind the soulful dark eyes that she now knew had the indisputable power to make her melt whenever he trained them on her, Grace had glimpsed a man who had had his fair share of heartache too, and she longed to discover the truth about that and perhaps to somehow ease some of his pain.

But she hadn't forgotten the river of icy shock that had cascaded through her bloodstream when he'd hauled her to her feet and said, 'You deserve to be severely punished for that.' *Her drunken ex-boyfriend Chris had said something similar that horrible evening.*

Of course Marco had only been teasing, but somehow his innocent action had unleashed the frightening memory of that devastating incident, and now it made her wonder again if she would ever be able to enjoy intimacy with a man without being afraid. She prayed that she would… More than that, she was *determined* that she would.

When Marco suggested that they should leave, Grace was honestly relieved. Not for want of trying, she had endeavoured to converse with the other guests at their table, but it had quickly become apparent that the social and material gulf between them was *vast*—too vast to be bridged even at a so-called 'relaxed' social function like this. How could she relate to a vacuous conversation that centred primarily round yachts, private planes and the latest Paris fashion trends? *It was a joke.* To be honest, she was genuinely sorry that they had such empty lives, with nothing other than the fruits of their material wealth and the desire for more of the same to occupy their minds.

Heading back to Marco's villa in the luxurious confines of his car, after a second flurry of paparazzi interest at the gates as they drove out, they both fell quiet. Had the desire he'd expressed to have her spend the rest of her holiday with him dissipated in light of the now obvious fact that Grace clearly didn't gel in any way with the elite social set that he moved in? If he now wanted her to leave then it would make it hard for her to accept the cheque he'd made out to the charity—not because she didn't greatly desire them to have it, but simply because she would feel that she'd let him down in some way.

'Marco…?'

Their gazes met and locked at the same time. A knowing smile raised the corners of her companion's sculpted lips. 'Please don't tell me that you now have reservations about our arrangement. I know the garden party must have been extremely tedious for you, and it was wrong of me to imagine that you might enjoy it, but for the rest of the day I will let *you* decide what we will do. Just name it and I will endeavour to make it happen. Any ideas?'

Stunned that he wanted her to stay, Grace stared. 'I thought—I thought that you'd had enough of me,' she lifted her shoulders in a painfully self-conscious shrug. 'You must have seen that I was like a fish out of water at lunch? I didn't have anything remotely in common with any of those people.'

'And I thank God that you didn't, Grace. But if you believe that you have nothing they might admire or want then I have to tell you that you're *wrong*. Why do you think that they were practically falling over themselves to tell you about their expensive toys and hobbies? I will tell you why: it was because they wanted to impress you. When they didn't get the reaction they wanted it probably made them feel quite insecure and jealous.'

'I can't believe that... Jealous of what?'

Marco sighed and combed his fingers through his hair. 'Your ability to simply be yourself...your *innocence*... You radiate the kind of goodness and beauty that money can't buy, and that's unsettling to people who believe they have it all.' His gaze intensified a little as he observed her, as though a slow fire simmered behind it. 'And I have definitely *not* had enough of you, *meu anjo*. Nowhere *near* enough.'

The water was deliciously and delightfully cool after the heat of the day. As Grace swam lap after lap of the azure marble-edged pool in the opulent villa she sensed the tension that she'd been holding in her body fall away and some measure of peace return. Marco had readily concurred when she'd told him she'd really like to go for a swim, and her pleasure at his agreement had soared when he'd shown her the beautiful outdoor pool in a secluded section of the landscaped gardens that she hadn't visited yet.

It was lucky that she'd had the presence of mind to bring her swimsuit, she thought, even though Marco had informed her that there was a large selection of swimming costumes in one of the guest rooms upstairs—just in case any visitors were bereft of one. But Grace was very glad of her one-piece suit. She'd bought in it in last year's spring sale, from a local department store that was part of a popular UK chain. The colour was a deep royal blue, and it had a bodice that wasn't cut too low and a high back. In truth, she felt *safe* in it. She certainly hadn't bought it because it was fashionable or might attract attention to her figure. Just the thought was anathema to her.

When Inês had briefly appeared at the poolside to tell Marco that he had an important phone call, Grace had been relieved, because it had meant she'd been able to get changed in private behind the poolside screen and quickly slip into the water before he got back.

After a while she stopped swimming, preferring to float on her back, her hands lightly paddling the azure water to keep her buoyant.

'You look like a mythical mermaid that's floated up from under the sea to grace the world with her beauty and remind us that magic still exists.'

The captivating male voice not only startled Grace, but made her turn upright in a hurry. She spluttered a little, because the sudden uncoordinated movement had sent a wave of water splashing into her face and she'd accidentally swallowed some.

Marco dropped to his haunches by the side of the pool, with his elbows resting on the knees of his elegant chinos and his long fingers loosely entwined. His dark hair gleamed bronze in the late-afternoon sunshine, and the strongly defined contours of his handsome face looked relaxed...*amused,* even. All of a sudden Grace was terribly self-conscious. How could she *not* be, in comparison to that vision of perfectly sculpted masculine beauty gazing back at her?

'I'm sure I look more like a drowned rat after that,' she quipped, as some sopping wet strands of hair strayed into her eyes and her long bedraggled ponytail plastered itself heavily against her shoulder.

'Don't put yourself down. You look nothing of the sort.'

'Well, you always look so effortlessly turned out and perfect. It's bound to make even the most confident girl feel a little insecure!'

'So I look perfect, do I?'

Before Grace even had an inkling of what he was going to do, Marco stood up, kicked off his shoes, then jumped fully clothed into the pool. Even as she stared at him in abject disbelief he started swimming towards her in an easy front crawl. Stopping in front of her, he smoothed back his seal-wet dark hair and disarmed her even more with the sexiest smile she'd ever seen.

'You're crazy...' she husked.

'If I am it's because that's how you make me feel when I'm with you.'

By the time his hands had settled round her hips under the water Grace's blood was already on fire with the need to have him touch her. When his beautiful mouth hungrily and a little roughly claimed hers *she* became a little bit crazy too...

CHAPTER SEVEN

As Marco's hands followed the slim yet curvaceous lines of Grace's body in the clinging wet swimsuit he didn't care that a moment of sheer uncharacteristic madness had prompted him to jump into the pool like that. All he knew was that expecting him to be further away from this woman than touching distance was akin to expecting him to comply with the near *impossible*.

Kissing her was the greatest sensual delight he had ever experienced, he'd discovered. She had a mouth that was made for long, drugging kisses that suspended time...could even make him forget his own name if he'd let it. Being with her, knowing that she had such a pure and giving heart, honestly made Marco feel like a better man. Instead of making him tread water in a pool of sharks, as he'd done for so long to make it in business and elevate himself far above his humble beginnings, fate had unexpectedly gifted him with the most beautiful golden-haired mermaid to remind him of other very important human needs. Needs such as the company of a woman whose presence and beauty he genuinely enjoyed and appreciated. And those qualities had become even sweeter now Marco knew he desired her too.

Twisting his mouth away from hers, he tugged down the soaking wet straps of Grace's swimsuit to expose her pert, duskily tipped breasts. The river of flame that was already flowing straight to his loins ensured that he didn't have a prayer of resisting the erotic temptation they presented. His mouth captured one, drawing the rigid velvet nipple deep inside, whilst his hand cupped and stroked the other. His heart leapt when, with a soft moan, Grace slid her fingers through the damp strands of his hair to keep him there.

Several mindless seconds later, when Marco honestly thought he might explode with the longing to be inside her, to join his painfully aroused body to hers in the most uninhibited and feral way, he lifted his head to capture her lips in another ravenously hungry kiss. His heart started to gallop in alarm when he sensed her stiffen, just as if she wanted to draw away, and gazing down into her shimmering blue eyes he saw a reticence he hadn't expected. The panicked look of dread that he'd witnessed earlier at the garden party, when he'd grabbed her up from the grass to tease her playfully, had not resurfaced—thank God—yet neither was she totally at ease.

He hadn't guessed wrongly about her intentions. She was already pulling her costume's straps back over her shoulders and tugging up the front of her suit to cover herself.

'What's wrong?' His fingers fastened round her chin to lift it higher and make her look at him.

'I just—I just need us to take things more slowly.'

Marco swore. He couldn't help it. It was his own damn fault, but he was in a near *agony* of lustful need.

Then he saw the glitter of moisture in Grace's eyes— saw one lone teardrop hug the side of her cheek as it tracked slowly down her face. He took in a deep, steadying breath. *She was afraid*, he thought incredulously. His chest welling with compassion—because it dawned on him that a man must have treated her badly, perhaps even hurt her *physically* somewhere along the line—he followed the trail of moisture with the pad of his thumb. *What he wouldn't give to meet the bastard that had hurt her and teach him a lesson that he'd never forget!*

'It's all right, my angel,' he soothed. 'I wouldn't dream of forcing you to do anything you don't want to do or aren't ready to do. That's a promise. I guess that something happened before with a guy? Will you tell me about it?'

Her hand resting lightly against the hip of his sodden chinos under the water, Grace stared back into Marco's arresting and compassionate dark gaze, knowing without a doubt that—aroused as he undoubtedly was—he wasn't the kind of man who would dream of taking cruel advantage of a woman…not like her drunken ex had tried to do.

It was only fair that she gave him an explanation. She hadn't exactly tried to stop him from becoming amorous—not when she had been equally turned on. It had only been when she'd realised where his passionate kisses and inflammatory touches were leading that Grace had suddenly felt overwhelmed. She wasn't afraid of Marco mistreating her, but after Chris's brutal assault it had become increasingly hard to trust a man to be tender with her feelings and wishes where her body was concerned… *any* man. Even a man she found she desperately wanted.

She sucked in a breath, smoothing back her hair with a tremulous hand. 'My ex-boyfriend tried to rape me.'

Marco's eyes glowered with fury as he bit out a curse in Portuguese. 'Did you call the police? Was he punished for such an assault?'

'He was drunk at the time, much more drunk than I realised, and—no…I didn't call the police. I was just so relieved that I was able to stop him.'

'How long ago was the attack?'

'About two years ago now.'

'And you have not been with a man since?'

Her cheeks flushed pink. 'No…I haven't.'

Marco reached out and tenderly stroked her cheek. 'You are young and beautiful, Grace. Please don't let the actions of one insensitive and unintelligent animal like him spoil your right to intimacy…nor your *enjoyment* of it.'

Entranced by his desire to console her, she nodded. Instead of being angry—perhaps believing that she'd led him on—Marco had reacted to the halting of their lovemaking with understanding and kindness. Deep inside she sensed the spell he'd already cast on her senses and on her heart becoming even more compelling, like a silken web it was hard to disentangle herself from.

'I'm doing my best to forget what happened—I really am… But it's not easy.'

For a long moment he stayed quiet, his hands lightly firming on her arms. 'I understand that,' he began, 'and I want you to know that whilst it is hard for me to be patient…when I find myself so passionately attracted to you…I will *learn* to be, because I believe that you are worth the wait.'

'Maybe—maybe we could try again later?' she suggested softly. The deeply carnal ache inside her was flaring more strongly now he was being so chivalrous and understanding of her hesitancy.

He nodded slowly, lowered his head towards her, then took possession of her surprised open mouth with a teasing erotic kiss, his tongue dancing with hers. As he started to withdraw, his teeth trapped her plump lower lip and nipped it slightly.

'Maybe we could,' he agreed, with a husky catch in

his voice that sounded like smoke and whisky. 'But right now I should get out of these wet clothes and dry myself. I am expecting a visit from my secretary very soon, to drop off some mail and give me an update on things. It shouldn't take long, as I've told everyone I'm taking a break, but we will have to confer in private for a while. There is a pile of towels over there on the lounger, and a robe. Behind those trees—can you see that low white roof?—is a changing facility for guests. You should be able to find everything you need in there, including a shower and hairdryer. When you're ready go and sit out on the patio outside the drawing room and Inês will get you a drink. Whatever happens we will have an enjoyable evening together, I promise.'

Turning away and swimming back to the edge of the pool, he hauled himself out, padded across to the lounger in his sopping wet clothes and, without so much as a backward glance at Grace, still treading water, stripped off in front of her without a care. He dried himself roughly with one of the towels, wound it round his lean, hard middle, then strolled back across the grass to the archway that led outside the garden to the back of the house.

Knowing the arresting sight of his bronzed and toned naked body was likely going to be imprinted on her memory *for ever,* and remembering the hotly carnal sensation of his mouth suckling at her breast, Grace released a long, stunned breath and then swam slowly across to the other end of the pool.

Dressed once again in the red and white maxi, she dried her hair and re-did her light make-up. By the time she started to walk barefoot back across the white marble flagstones surrounding the pool the sun was setting. It was a given that she had to stop to view one of the world's

most breathtaking displays of natural beauty—especially
when the dazzling globe so dramatically dominated the
horizon, its siena rays bleeding hauntingly into the dark-
ening blue sky. She felt a near-overwhelming desire for
Marco to be standing beside her, so that they might enjoy
the sight together, and there was a strange emptiness inside Grace because he wasn't.

After a time she walked on, idly wondering what his
secretary was like and hoping that she wouldn't deprive
Grace of his company for long.

She was heading down the long marbled corridor to
the drawing room when she heard Inês open the front
doors to invite Marco's visitor inside. It surprised her
to hear an English accent. The woman who spoke to
the housekeeper greeted her with affection and pleasure
in her tone. Her voice sounded cultured and kind, and
the little knot of anxiety at the pit of Grace's stomach
blessedly unravelled. After sitting amongst the snobbish
guests at Francesca Bellini's garden party it was nice to
know that Marco's secretary was not cut from the same
superior and condescending cloth.

Curious to put a face to the lovely voice, she slowly
retraced her steps to the other end of the corridor and,
rounding it, stole a peek at the attractive middle-aged
woman with dark blonde wavy hair cut flatteringly just
above her shoulders. Dressed in a smart but understated
dove-grey linen suit, she carried a slim dark brown brief-
case down by her side, and although she was clearly having a meeting with Marco she might have just as easily
been meeting friends for coffee or dinner, such was her
relaxed and amiable yet undoubtedly elegant stance.

She was still smiling and talking to Inês when she
registered Grace's presence. Her initial look of surprise
turned to another pleased smile as she skirted round the

housekeeper to walk towards her. She held out her hand. 'You must be Grace. I've been so looking forward to meeting you. I'm Martine—Marco's secretary.'

Her warm clasp was just as friendly as her manner, and Grace gave her an unreserved smile back. 'It's nice to meet you, Martine. Have you had to travel very far to get here?'

She laughed, 'Good heavens, no! I'm staying at one of my boss's hotels just up the road. Wherever he is in the world Marco likes to have me nearby. The man is constantly working, and invariably so am I. But now that he's told me he's actually taking a short holiday, after our meeting I'll have a few days off to take a break myself. I'm going to pop back to London, to my little house I very rarely get to see, and I can't tell you how much I'm looking forward to it!'

'I'm from London too,' Grace volunteered.

'I know. Marco told me. He also tells me that you've been out to Africa to help take care of orphaned children?'

'That's right. I work for a charity that's dedicated specifically to that cause.'

'I'm in admiration of you doing that, Grace. There's not many beautiful young women like you who would choose such a worthy but distinctly unglamorous career... which is a great shame, in my opinion.'

'It wasn't a hard choice, believe me. The unconditional love that those children radiate—even in the worst of circumstances—makes it easy.'

'Well, now that I've met you I can see why Marco has decided to take a holiday at last. I owe you a big thank-you for that. You know he almost *never* takes a break?'

Grace was still smiling at the other woman when the pair of twin doors to the side of the vast reception area opened and Marco appeared. She didn't miss the quiz-zical little frown that creased his brow when he saw that she was chatting with his secretary.

'Martine. I didn't know that you'd arrived. How are you? Do you have everything that you need at the hotel? They're looking after you?'

'Hello, Marco. I'm fine, thank you. And although they shouldn't the staff at the hotel are waiting on me hand, foot and finger. I couldn't want for anything. I've just been introducing myself to your lovely friend.'

He only spared her the briefest glance in acknowledge-ment, but for Grace it was like being touched by living electricity and she tingled all the way down to the edges of her toes.

'Good,' he replied perfunctorily, pushing one of the twin doors opened a little wider. 'Why don't you come into my study and make yourself comfortable? Inês, can you please bring us some coffee?'

'Of course, *senhor*.'

As the housekeeper turned to go about her duties, and Martine bade goodbye to Grace and went through to the study, Marco immediately came over to join her. It hit Grace just then that he looked much more like the quint-essential movie star than Lincoln Roberts could ever as-pire to look. With his bronzed skin, sexy dark eyes and fitted black shirt and jeans, he exuded an effortless and brooding sexuality that made Grace's stomach clench and her legs go weak.

'You found everything that you needed poolside?' he asked, his cool fingers gently tilting her chin towards him.

'The changing room couldn't have been better fitted out than a suite at the Ritz! Not that I've ever *been* to the Ritz,' she added quickly.

Marco chuckled. 'One day I will take you to stay there, if you like?'

'I wasn't suggesting that I wanted to—'

'I know you weren't. But just indulge the fantasy that I might take you there one day, hmm?'

'I'd better let you get to your meeting with Martine. She seems like a very nice woman, by the way.'

'She is. She's also very efficient and intuitive when it comes to what I need at work. I told you—I only ever employ the very best people.' He deliberately let his gaze fall into Grace's eyes.

Transfixed, she stared back at him, more than a little excited that soon they would be alone together, with no one to think of or to please but themselves.

Marco lowered his voice. 'Wait for me out on the patio. This shouldn't take very long.'

As Grace returned to the elegant drawing room and walked out onto the patio she couldn't help praying and hoping that it really *wouldn't* be too long before Marco was able to join her. She was more at ease now that she had met the very warm and down-to-earth Martine, and she had been quietly gratified when she'd told her that her boss rarely took a break from work—her observation definitely suggesting that he was taking one now because of Grace's influence.

She breathed in the sultry evening air and breathed out again, jettisoning any further worries and concerns that might prey on her peace of mind to concentrate instead on enjoying the last few minutes of the spectacular sunset…

Soft lighting dotted at various strategic points round the patio automatically illuminated the area as the sun went down, and at the same time made the quarter-moon that hung in the sky seem magically brighter. The slightly chill caress of a passing breeze made her shiver. The air was no longer quite so sultry. Grace wished that she'd brought a wrap or a stole to drape round her shoulders. But that morning—along with the straw hat that she'd left behind—it had been the furthest thing from her mind.

Rising from her chair, she glanced over at the still open French doors leading back into the drawing room. A sudden doubt seized her. *What was she doing?* She really ought to be thinking about going home. Marco might be ages yet. What if after his meeting with Martine *work* dominated his mind? Maybe so much so that he wouldn't want to spend the evening relaxing with Grace?

Recalling the look in his eyes when he'd told her that his meeting wouldn't take long, and realising that she was probably being ridiculous, she breathed out a slightly more reassured breath and resolved to think about something else. But her mind seemed intent on revisiting the subject of Marco working too hard and rarely taking a break.

She was acutely aware that she was feeling unusually protective of a man whom the world undoubtedly viewed as incredibly fortunate and privileged, who surely didn't have the same ordinary wants and needs of most humans—such as the need to slow down sometimes and take stock, or the desire for a loving relationship, supportive family and friends and children of his own? From time to time, when he'd unwittingly let down his guard a little and referred to his orphaned upbringing, Grace had glimpsed both hurt and loneliness in Marco's eyes and it had made her insides knot in sympathy…

'*Senhorita?*'

Inês stood in the doorway between the drawing room and the patio, a polite but warm smile on her broad open face. 'Senhor Aguilar asked me to tell you that he will not be much longer now. He also asked me to prepare you some refreshments while you are waiting for him. I have served them in the courtyard garden. Can you come with me, please?'

With little notion of the delights awaiting her, Grace was happy to follow the friendly housekeeper down the long marbled corridor then through an airy vestibule that lead out onto a stunning sunken courtyard filled with lemon trees. In a private corner of the enchanting area a small wrought-iron table was laid with an array of appetising snacks, plus a beautiful crystal decanter of red wine accompanied by two matching glasses. The gently atmospheric lighting was provided by several pretty lanterns with candles flickering inside them. There was no evidence of a breeze here at all. Instead the air was sultry and still again, and the only sound to break the silence was the repetitive shrill of cicadas that Grace was becoming more and more accustomed to.

She turned to regard Inês smilingly. 'This is wonderful. *Obrigado*… Thank you…thank you so much.'

The other woman beamed. 'Enjoy,' she said, then left her alone.

It wasn't the same eating alone…it wasn't the same at all. Although she'd made a valiant attempt at eating some of the delicious food, Grace realised it was almost impossible for her to enjoy it when her insides were seized with nervous tension because Marco was taking so long. Time seemed to pass agonisingly slowly, and when he still didn't appear the tension inside her turned into full-blown anxiety that something must be wrong.

Had Martine perhaps brought bad news?

She had just decided she could no longer sit still and wait—she would go in search of her host herself to make sure nothing was amiss—when he appeared in the arched doorway. Its elegant stucco designs were just about visible beneath the heavy fall of red bougainvillaea that draped over it.

In the instant that she registered his arrival Grace detected a certain weariness and strain in his demeanour that made her heart race with concern. Before she knew it, she'd rushed towards him to clasp his hand. The hooded dark eyes that were so incredibly compelling flashed in surprise. When surprise turned to indisputable pleasure her heart raced not with concern but for a very different reason indeed.

He didn't loosen her hand, or berate her for being so presumptuous, as had been her fear. In fact, he used it as leverage to impel her towards him. The sheer unadulterated joy of being near him again, of scenting his provocative cologne and feeling the heat that radiated from his body, went way *beyond* simple pleasure. The contact that she'd been longing for far exceeded all her imaginative secret hopes.

'Is everything okay? I was worried,' she admitted softly.

'Worried...about me?' Marco's deep rich voice bordered on being amazed. 'Why?'

'I was worried in case Martine had brought you some bad news, or—or that you had to get back to work for some reason and I wouldn't see you tonight after all. I'd have been seriously upset about that, because it's becoming more and more obvious that you work too hard and clearly need some time off.'

Disconcertingly, he chuckled. 'I've had no bad news, and neither do I need to get back to work. Is that why you've suddenly appeared in my life, Grace? To make sure that I don't overdo things and work too hard?'

'I'm sorry if I sometimes speak my mind a bit too much.'

'Never apologise for being honest—trust me, it is far better than being lied to. Now, you can tell me the truth about something else… You told me that you were exhausted when you came back from Africa, and this morning you overslept. Are you feeling any better now? If you need to see a doctor I can arrange it…even tonight, if need be?'

'I'm honestly fine. I definitely don't need to see a doctor. But thanks for being so kind and asking.'

'Well, seeing as we are both absolutely fine, I think we can now relax and enjoy our evening together, no?' He lifted a dark eyebrow. 'Do you know, I can't remember the last time anyone worried about me?'

The shrug of his broad shoulders when he said that was almost matter-of-fact…but the expression Grace saw in his eyes was anything *but*. That was the moment when she knew she couldn't—*wouldn't*—deny him anything.

'Well, then.' Gently tugging her hand free, hardly knowing what possessed her, she boldly traced the outline of his fascinating lips with her fingertips. 'If that's the case, then your friends can't know what a special man they have in their lives.'

'If you persist in saying such things to me…and touching me like that…then my promise to you to be patient will make a liar of me—because I won't be able to keep it,' he confessed, gravel-voiced.

'Then don't.' She knew her transfixed stare devoured him, because her need to have him hold her right then, *to make love to her*, was so intense that Grace couldn't begin to curtail it. It was akin to a swollen river about to burst its banks.

'What?'

'Don't keep your promise. I no longer want you to. Be patient, I mean. Remember I asked you in the pool if we could try again later?' she breathed in a velvet-voiced whisper.

He muttered something that sounded like the kind of curse a man might make when he'd been tested to the extremes of his endurance, and the ensuing kiss that claimed her lips was so hot, hard and hungry that Grace knew she didn't have a hope of holding onto her balance. But at that moment she didn't even *care*. Neither did she mind that the passionate caress was completely devoid of tenderness or finesse, because she knew it was driven by an elemental power strong enough and raw enough to knock her right off of her feet.

As a woman who had never experienced being desired with such hungry intent before, and who had never wanted a man more, in the most carnal way, she found Marco's attentions more welcome than stunning cool rain on a baking hot desert that hadn't seen the like for months. With no guilt whatsoever, she allowed herself to luxuriate freely in them, feeling nothing but gratitude...

The rough scrape of the chiselled jaw that was already displaying a five o'clock shadow and the scalding sensual demand of his lips and tongue stoked such a fire in her that in the future, when this incredible hiatus with him came to an end, she knew she would be deaf, dumb and blind to the attractions of any other man.

Breathing hard as he tore his mouth away from hers, Marco lifted his head so that he could study her. At the same time, his hands tightened possessively round her hips. 'Are you telling me that you will let me take you to bed?'

'You mean...right now?' Grace knew her question inflamed him, because she saw the molten heat that was already in his eyes flare passionately, like a fire that had just been doused in petrol.

'*Querido Deus!* Yes, *now*…before this constant craving for you drives me completely out of my mind.'

Firming his arm possessively round her waist, he urgently guided her out of the arched courtyard like a man indisputably on a mission…

CHAPTER EIGHT

WITH his heart beating a throbbing tattoo inside his chest, Marco held onto Grace's small slender hand and led her into his vast bedroom. The twin glass doors onto the wrought-iron balcony were open and a scented breeze blew in from the gardens below, making the cream-coloured voile drapes dance.

The heat that his body was gripped by hadn't cooled in any way, but Marco couldn't help remembering his vow to seduce Grace 'subtly and artfully' and not rush her. Especially when she had confided in him that her despicable ex-boyfriend had assaulted her. But the moment she turned her big blue eyes on him, and he saw her pretty, full upper lip quiver gently, every thought in his head disappeared except the one that urged him to love her long into the night…

'Won't Inês wonder where we've gone?' she asked. 'We just abandoned all the lovely food she'd prepared and came up here.'

'My housekeeper has four children…she's a woman of the world. I don't think she will wonder for very long about where we've gone, Grace.'

'Oh.'

'All I care about is that we are alone at last. We can

forget about the rest of the world for a while and just concentrate on ourselves…agreed?'

'Yes…all right.'

She visibly shivered as Marco calmly started to undo the buttons on her red and white bodice. But if he gave the impression of being calm and in control then he definitely *wasn't*. It took every ounce of will he possessed to control the trembling in his fingers as he finished unfastening the buttons on her dress and helped her to step out of it. The prim swimsuit she'd worn in the pool had done its best to disguise the allure of her shapely form—and he had to say it had failed—but the lacy pink strapless bra that she wore now, along with matching cotton panties, *didn't*. The word *exquisite*, used to describe a beautiful woman, was sometimes overused in his book…but he had no argument with the description in the present case. Grace's body was slender and supple, but her figure also curved in and out like an hourglass, and her beautiful skin was flawlessly pale and smooth and instantly invited his touch.

Skimming his fingertips below her breastbone and down to her sexy little bellybutton, he held her wide-eyed gaze with a slow, teasing smile. 'I was right,' he said.

'Right about what, exactly?'

'That underneath that not-so-effective disguise of an "ordinary" girl that you frequently like to insist you are there resides the bewitching body of a very hot temptress indeed.'

Blushing helplessly, she knew her glance was adorably shy as she observed him. 'I don't think so.'

'Yes, I think so,' he insisted, chuckling softly. 'But, as alluring as your pretty underwear undoubtedly is, I'm afraid I'm going to have to divest you of it if I want to accomplish what I have in mind right now.'

'And that is…?'

'To make love to you all through the night.'

The edges of her straight white teeth clamped nervously down onto her vulnerable lower lip. Glancing over at the emperor-sized bed with its oyster silk bedlinen and luxurious pillows and cushions, her soft cheeks bloomed again with the delicate pink of a summer rose. 'That bed seems an awfully long way away,' she commented, a distinct catch in her voice.

'Not if I carry you there.'

There was something deliciously wicked and decadent about being transported across such a palatial room to an equally opulent bed covered in the finest silk by her handsome would-be lover. Indeed, Grace could have been forgiven for thinking she was dreaming the whole thing—except that the experience was light years away from any seduction her imagination could have contrived, even in the throes of the most erotic dream.

By the time Marco had lain her carefully down on the bed, kicked off his shoes and stripped down to his black silk boxers, she was shivering so hard with longing, anticipation and not a little apprehension that all she could do was stare mutely up at him. In her mind she silently paid homage to his beauty—the strong, clean lines of his hard-muscled shoulders and torso, the slim masculine hips and silkily hirsute powerful thighs—then automatically returned her gaze to his compelling, strong-boned visage to linger on his mouth…a mouth that could so easily have been sculpted by an Italian Renaissance artist it was so sublime. Lifting her glance higher, she fell into the seductive beam of depthless dark eyes that she already knew could make her dissolve with barely any effort at all.

'I want you to sit up and kiss me,' he told her, the usually resonant voice pitched a little lower because it was infused with desire.

Mesmerised, caught up in a hypnotic spell she knew she would never forget after this night, Grace did as he asked. Marco immediately circled her chest to unhook the fastening at the back of her flimsy lace bra. As soon as her breasts were freed, and she experienced the gossamer caress of warm air glancing against her skin, he claimed her lips in another long, melting kiss. After the initial urgent clash of teeth and tongues, the sensual quality of their mutual exploration of each other was akin to being bathed in moonlight and honey. As she lay down against the luxurious covers of the bed Grace knew it was a tantalising gateway to what was to follow.

When Marco planted his strong thighs either side of her, then bent his head once more to kiss and suckle her breasts, her body was seized by another bout of irresistible shivering.

'This is not your first time…is it?' Immediately he raised his head to examine her, his glance both searching and concerned.

Moistening her lips with her tongue, Grace nervously held his gaze. 'No. But I've only been with a man once before…when I lost my virginity.'

The unhappy memory of the occasion made her tense briefly. It had only happened because her university boyfriend had pressured her and the following day he told her he regretted it because there was another girl he liked more, and their fledgling relationship had come to an abrupt and *humiliating* end. So far, her experience of intimacy had not been great. But until now no other man she'd ever met had stirred the kind of powerful feelings inside her that Marco did. Instinctively she knew that making love with him would be wonderful...*more* than wonderful.

Making no comment, but with a provocative half-smile playing about his lips, he moved his hands down to her hips to remove the rest of her lacy underwear. Sucking in her breath, Grace held onto his toned bronzed biceps as he went about the sensuous task, her body trembling even more. He touched his mouth to the flat plane of her stomach, and her hands automatically fell away as he planted light but explosive little kisses all over its surface. When his lips moved lower down, and he began to kiss the delicate sensitive skin covering her slender inner thighs, she turned her head to the silk pillow behind her, closed her eyes, and willingly allowed the tide of heat that was building unstoppably inside to hold sway, fervently wishing that it might go on for ever...

As if intuiting her need, Marco let his hot silken tongue explore her more intimately, and suddenly the ability to think at all was replaced by a profound willingness to surrender, to allow this intoxicating pleasure to take her wherever it would. Grace no longer tried to still the trembling that grew more and more prevalent with every seductive volcanic touch that Marco delivered. It was a natural reaction, she realised, simply part of the erotic interplay between them. And suddenly the building storm of sensation inside her became molten lightning, an electrical conflagration bar none that had her totally at its mercy. Once again, all she could do was surrender. At the peak of the waves that flowed through her she cried out, then lay dazed and shivering as the torrid heat slowly started to ebb.

Marco's hypnotic voice murmured something that she didn't quite hear, and her eyes flew opened as she sensed his body moving over hers. She saw that he too was naked now. Her heart began to thump hard. His eyes crinkled at the corners as he bestowed a sexy smile down upon her.

She reached out to touch her palm to his beard-roughened jaw and he turned his mouth towards it and kissed her there. 'That was amazing,' she told him softly.

'It was amazing for me too. I fear I am becoming addicted to you, Grace… To your scent and to your touch. No matter how much you give me…I'm afraid I just want more.'

Sensing the tension in his body as he held himself above her, Grace instinctively raised her legs so that they clasped his slim, arrow-straight hips in a sensual vice. As she registered the uninhibited look of gratification on his face another ecstatic moan was punched from her lungs, and he plunged himself deep inside her. He stilled for a long moment, so that they both received the maximum enjoyment from the contact, their gazes meeting and locking in mutual wonderment as they did so. When Marco started to rock back and forth inside her she hungrily sought his lips, kissing him with the kind of passion and ardour that she'd never even guessed she might be capable of. Her own eager responses were a revelation to her.

And now, as her lover moved with even more ardour and intent inside her, the place the hard, scalding pleasure of his possession was taking her to started to imitate the electrical storm she'd succumbed to earlier, and she found herself tumbling into it without restraint, the ecstatic sensations that gripped her growing more and more wildly urgent. She buried her face in the warm sanctuary between Marco's neck and shoulder as she flew free. At the same time tears flowed into her eyes and spilled over down her cheeks. Just before he thrust even deeper he wound his fingers through her hair, pulled back her head and kissed her hard. Then, with a helpless guttural groan, he too flew free…

The pounding wasn't just inside his heart but in his head too, Marco acknowledged in alarm as he rolled onto his side, breathing hard. The shocking realisation of what he'd just done hit him like a hammer-blow. *Had he somehow lost his mind?* Dear God! He'd just made love to Grace without even the merest thought of protecting her. He'd been so caught up in the maelstrom of need and desire that had deluged him he'd simply lost the ability to think straight. It just hadn't been possible.

'Marco? Are you all right?'

He turned to regard the matchless blue eyes that were considering him so concernedly. A rueful smile hijacked his lips as he cupped her small delicately made jaw. 'Yes, I'm all right—although after what I've just experienced that may well be the understatement of the year. But I also have to confess to being somewhat stunned by my recklessness. I should have used protection, but I got so swept away by you…by what was happening between us…that I didn't. I hardly know what to say, Grace, except to tell you that I'm genuinely sorry.'

'I'm equally to blame. I got just as carried away as you, Marco. If anything happens as a result of this I want to reassure you that I won't take you to court to get your money…well…at least not *all* of your money.'

This was said in such a matter-of-fact tone that it took Marco a couple of seconds to realise that she was shamelessly teasing him. For a sickening moment the soul-destroying belief that had hounded most of his existence—that people only befriended him for what they could get out of him—had disturbingly revisited him. It didn't help his case right then to remember his ex-girlfriend's misguided and heartless attempt to try and fleece him to help fund her expensive drug habit.

'Don't even *joke* about that,' he growled. 'In all seriousness…if you *were* to fall pregnant with my child then of course you could rely on me to help you in any way that I can. You certainly wouldn't have to resort to taking me to court for child support! But from now on I will definitely be more careful when we make love.'

Grace was silent, propping herself up on her elbows to study him. Any sign of humour had utterly vanished, he saw. In fact, her expression was almost grave.

'I'm not taking the possibility of falling pregnant, lightly Marco. I'm well aware that it's a life-changing thing, as well as a huge responsibility…to raise a child, I mean. It impacts on a woman's life like nothing else. But we've done what we've done and now we'll just have to wait and see. Can't we just enjoy what we have right now, or is that too selfish? We both work hard…we're both responsible people—don't you think we deserve to relax and not worry? We've agreed that we'll share this one holiday together then return to our own lives. From your reaction to my little joke I'm guessing that you've probably been deceived by women before, but you've nothing like that to fear from me. I'm a very up-front kind of girl, Marco. What you see is what you get. Whilst I'll always be more than grateful that you've agreed to help the children's charity, I don't want anything for myself other than your company…at least until the end of this holiday. After that I'll go back to London, return to my work and carry on as normal. I mean it. You won't even have to hear from me again if you don't want to.'

Icy fear hurtled through his veins. He caught hold of her slender-boned wrist with a sense of hard-to-suppress fury at the idea she would so easily turn her back on him and not have a single regret. 'And what if you *do* become pregnant?' he demanded. 'What then? Will you still insist on maintaining your distance from me?'

Pulling away from him, Grace rubbed her wrist with a wounded look in her eyes. Then she sighed and lay down on her side, resting her head against the silken pillows behind her. In the soft glow of the lamplight her fair hair tumbled like skeins of spun gold down over her bare shoulders. It was the only eye-catching adornment to her lovely nakedness, Marco reflected. He didn't doubt that he was a lucky man to see her like this…to be able to reach out his hand and touch that matchless skin whenever he chose…to hear her soft moans and cries when he made love to her again—which he fully intended to do, and *soon*.

'If it did turn out that I was pregnant, then of *course* I would let you know. But let me ask you something… Do you want to be a father, Marco?'

It was the hardest question he had ever been asked. His reaction to it sent a multitude of fears and hopes crashing through him. It was the hope that disturbed him the most. 'I have no experience of what it entails to be a father…no good example,' he admitted gravel-voiced. The weight of sorrow that suddenly lay on his chest was close to unbearable. Because he was so ill at ease and uncomfortable he batted the question back to Grace. 'What about you? Do you maybe harbour a secret desire to become a mother?'

Shrugging, she reached for a section of the silk eiderdown to pull up over her chest. 'One day, perhaps. But not yet…not while I'm still young and have the time and energy to help children who desperately need a home and a school to go to. Anyway…we're hypothesising about something that probably won't even happen.' As if she'd just thought of something more pressing, she turned her glance back to Marco. 'I know you were raised in an orphanage, but did you never see your father at all?'

Manoeuvring himself up into a sitting position, Marco deliberately averted his gaze from Grace's—even when she sat up next to him, dragging the silk covers with her. 'No. My father wasn't around and neither was my mother. She died giving birth to me, and my father couldn't handle taking care of me by himself, so he gave me away to an orphanage. Are you satisfied now that you've heard the whole sad and sorry story?'

'Oh, Marco.'

The compassion in her voice burst the dam of emotion he was intent on holding back...*had* been holding back for years. He turned his head to regard her furiously. 'Don't you *dare* feel sorry for me. If you do then I'll get Miguel to take you back to your villa right now and you will never see me again, I mean it! Do you understand?'

Mutely, she nodded.

Marco could hardly hear himself think beneath the drowning wave of rage and fear that crashed over him. He didn't want his past *or* his emotions put under the microscope by anybody...especially not Grace. The kindness in her eyes would likely tempt him to reveal things that would only end up making him feel bad. He might not have made peace with the events that had shaped him, but at least he'd kept their memory far enough at bay to get on with his life and become a success of sorts. *At least he wasn't dependent on anyone else to build his self-esteem.*

Just when he believed his emotions were returning to a more even keel, with her inimitable ability to speak her mind Grace stirred them up again.

'It's not that I feel sorry for you, you know. It just

grieves me that you might believe you're not deserving of sympathy or care. At least…that's the impression I get. You're such a good man, Marco. I can't believe—'

'I warned you, but you clearly didn't listen. Now you will have to go.'

He pushed his fingers furiously through his hair, his heart thumping. At the same time he wondered why he was being so reckless and self-destructive, depriving himself of the one good thing that had really started to matter to him. He'd done the same throughout his growing up in the orphanage. If anyone had tried to get close he'd pushed them away, fearing either that they didn't mean it or that he couldn't live up to any expectations they might have of him.

'What?'

'I said you will have to go. I warned you that I neither wanted nor welcomed your sympathy, but you had to persist, didn't you?'

'All right, then.'

Although her lovely blue eyes were silently assessing him, and no doubt reaching more unwanted conclusions about his vehement reaction, Grace was already throwing back the silk covers and moving towards the side of the bed. Dry-mouthed, Marco at last came to his senses and reached for her. Enfolding her from behind, he moved his hands over her bared breasts, kneading them, playing with the rigid velvet tips and pulling her urgently back against his chest. A river of volcanic heat stormed through his bloodstream and went straight to his loins. He had no recollection of ever being this hungry and mindlessly desirous for a woman before…he only knew that he needed her almost as much as he needed his next breath.

'I've changed my mind,' he breathed against the side

of her neck under the soft fall of her hair. 'I don't want you to go. It was stupid of me to say I did.'

She carefully disengaged his hands from her breasts and turned round to study him. Her smile was tender. 'I wouldn't have gone you know. I wouldn't have left you because I know you didn't really mean it. I would have just gone to look for Inês, asked her where the kitchen was, made a cup of tea and then sat out on the patio until you were ready to talk to me again.'

'Is that so?' He stared back at her in astonishment. Then he shook his head, leaned forward, and ravished her with a hotly exploring open-mouthed kiss. When her arms feverishly encircled his waist and she pressed herself so close to him that she felt like a part of him he'd never even known he'd lost he broke off the caress to gaze searchingly into her eyes. 'You are either very stubborn, Grace, or unbelievably daring that you would risk my fury in that way. Do you know I've heard that even some of my board members quake in their boots at the thought I might lose my temper if they displease me in some way?'

'You can't believe it's a *good* thing to intimidate people like that...surely?'

'*You* were not intimidated.'

'Yes, but I'm as stubborn as a mule...so my dad often tells me. Even if I'm terrified of something I somehow can't let it get the better of me. Except when my boyfriend attacked me,' she added thoughtfully. 'Afterwards, I let my fear of it happening again stop me from getting close to anyone...I regret that. But I'll never let fear have such a hold on me again.'

In all his years of doing business Marco had never met her equal, he mused in wonder. It was rare indeed that anyone stood up to him or was so frank in confessing their reflections. Grace wasn't just brave, she was inspirational too.

Quickly, his musings turned to much more urgent and seductive reflections as he saw the sexy evidence of his passionate exploration on her moist slightly swollen lips. 'I think we have done enough talking for now, don't you? We can resume this very interesting conversation later.'

'If you say so.'

She gave him the kind of cheekily provocative grin that came close to making him vocalise his need for her in the most basic and unequivocal terms available to him in language. Instead, he tipped her back onto the bed and demonstrated his need in a much more physical and satisfying way for them both...

It was rare that he stayed in bed all through the night with a woman and didn't get up early, to work or distance himself in some way. Telling himself that it was because he was on vacation, but knowing it was more, *much* more than that, Marco turned onto his side to view his still-sleeping lover. The oyster silk cover had slipped from her body and he silently studied the naked, very feminine curves of hip and supple thigh. Immediately the waves of strong desire that seemed to be a permanent occurrence whenever he was near Grace flowed forcefully through him again.

Drawing the cover up gently over her bared satin shoulder, he realised he couldn't seem to get enough of both her company *and* her body. When once again the thought struck him that he might have made her pregnant, he sensed a shockingly uncharacteristic surge of hope sweep into his heart. He had no family. *In his will he had left most of his considerable fortune to charity.* Not once in his romantic history had he ever considered marrying and starting a family of his own. But then he had never really been in love or cared for a woman enough to contemplate it.

Examining the face that was just as lovely in repose as when she was awake, Marco felt a definite quickening inside his chest. If he and Grace *did* make a child together, what would the infant be like? he wondered. He was suddenly fascinated by the idea. He was so dark—and she, being fair and blue-eyed, was his polar opposite. Smiling to himself, he lifted the silk coverlet again to contemplate her smooth flat abdomen. Mesmerised, he grazed his fingertips over the area just below her belly-button. Grace stirred and opened her eyes. It was like looking into the most sublime sunlit blue lake.

'What are you doing?' Her soft voice was sleepily husky.

Marco let the cover drop back down over her body. 'I was simply looking at you and marvelling at how beautiful you are.'

'Flattery will get you everywhere.'

'That's exactly what I hoped you say.'

'Except that I have a sudden urge to go for a swim… may I?'

Marco tugged down the covers he had just let fall back into place and employed the most seductive smile he could muster. 'After we have made love,' he told her.

Colouring a little, nonetheless Grace made no attempt to cover herself again. 'It's a good job that you're so fit, because you really are insatiable,' she murmured, even as her slender arms wound firmly round his neck.

CHAPTER NINE

WITH unashamed charm, Marco had persuaded Grace to allow him to take her shopping. Her agreement had only come about when she'd realised that all she had to wear was the dress she'd worn yesterday because she hadn't expected to be spending the night with him.

Just the thought of how ardently they had made love made her heart race anew, and all the places on her body where he had visited his amorous attentions throbbed and tingled at the memory. The deliciously disturbing sensations were heightened by the realisation that her feelings for this man went far beyond merely enjoying his company. At every turn he mesmerised and seduced her… just by virtue of being himself. Grace loved the sound of his accented voice…the extravagant way he gestured with his hands when explaining something…the flash of an unguarded smile that was more potent even than bright sunlight illuminating a cloudy day…

When she'd suggested that she return to her own villa for some fresh clothing, Marco had caught her by the waist and silenced her reasoning with a long, lingering kiss that had made any inclination to do anything else but be with him inexorably vanish. After that he'd directed her to a luxurious wet room, so that she could take a shower, while he made some arrangements for their shopping trip. Grace had quickly learned that there were always arrangements to be made whenever he ventured out—simply because he was so well known. She'd also intuited that public interest in his activities gave him little pleasure. It was simply a have-to-deal-with by-product of his phenomenal success.

Shortly after his own shower, Marco changed into fresh military-style chinos and another loose white shirt and appeared on the patio, where she was waiting for him.

With his dark hair gleaming, he was looking fresh-faced, unbelievably handsome and somehow endearingly boyish too. Whenever she recalled him angrily asking her if she was satisfied now that he'd told her the full 'sad and sorry' story of his upbringing, she sensed the shame he clearly still felt. She wanted to tell him that it was hardly *his* fault that his grieving father had left him there—that he deserved nothing but admiration for being able to transcend his challenging and tragic start in life to become the incredible success he was now. There should be no hint of shame whatsoever…he was an *inspiration*, Grace wanted to say.

The only problem was that their relationship wasn't yet on the kind of footing where she could demonstrate her understanding and compassion towards him without risking being angrily rebuffed. Having already experienced how swiftly Marco's defences had slammed into place when she'd been about to express her concern for what he'd endured, she knew she had to rein in her natural instinct to try and get him to talk about it more…at least until he was sure she wasn't going to betray him in any way.

'I see Inês has made you coffee?' he observed, smiling.

'Your housekeeper is a godsend. You're very lucky to have her.'

'You think I don't know that?'

'I don't doubt that you know it. You're probably ex-tremely appreciative of every person who works for you, if the truth be known. Likewise, they must be very ap-preciative of you,' she added brightly.

Frowning thoughtfully, Marco pulled out the chair op-posite her at the table. For a long moment he silently sur-veyed the stunning vista spread out before them. Already a shimmering haze of heat hung over it. 'Don't be in such a hurry to elevate me to Employer of the Year,' he ad-vised, helping himself to some coffee. 'I am not always so popular...particularly when it falls to me to make some of the tougher decisions. For instance when I have to let people go.'

'I expect that comes with the territory. In your position you're always looking at the bigger picture, aren't you? What's cost-effective and what's not etc. Did you always want to be a businessman?' Relaxing back into her chair, Grace offered Marco the little dish of sugar crystals, but with a slight shake of his head he declined it. She stirred another couple of crystals into her own beverage, grin-ning unrepentantly when he lifted an eyebrow.

'I see that you have a sweet tooth, Grace?'

'It's only a small vice. Anyway...you haven't answered my question.'

'My answer is no...I didn't always want to be a busi-nessman. I started out just wanting to play golf and to become good at it. There was a course not far from the orphanage...'

He winced—*but at least he wasn't avoiding mention-ing it*, Grace thought. She almost held her breath at what she couldn't help but see as a breakthrough.

'When I turned fifteen,' he continued, 'I got a job there, collecting all the stray golf balls. One of the members befriended me. He asked me to be his caddy. He also started to teach me how to play. After a while, I did indeed become good at the game.'

'But you didn't want to take it up as a career?'

His dark eyes silently assessed her before he replied, as if he was not quite sure she was being serious. 'You have never looked up my name on the internet and read my bio?'

Slightly bewildered, Grace swallowed hard. 'No, I haven't. Should I have?'

'I was what they call a scratch golfer…good enough to turn professional. I did indeed have a very successful career in the game for a few years, and won several trophies. But then I started to see that the men and women who owned the prestigious courses we played on made even more money the professional players. That was when I decided on a change of career, and became the businessman and property developer that I am today.'

'And there are no regrets about leaving your golfing career behind? I mean, do you equally enjoy what you do now?'

He smiled. 'I do. Especially when it brings me into unexpected contact with a smart, stubborn, pretty woman like you, Grace…a woman who will risk everything—even being detained by my security guards—to help further a cause she believes in.'

She was still reeling from his admiring words when Marco strode round the table and urged her to her feet.

'Mmm, you smell nice,' she told him, even as her heart leapt at his nearness.

'You always say what you're thinking, don't you?' he remarked, looking amused.

'Do you think that's a bad trait?'

'I'm not saying that at all. But I can see how it could get you into trouble.'

Grace frowned. 'I know... But I never say anything horrible or harsh to offend anyone.'

'I believe you. You are far too well-meaning and kind for that.' He tweaked her earlobe, then brushed her lips with a brief kiss. 'But what if I were to adopt the same approach? What if I told you exactly what *I* was thinking right now, hmm?'

Her legs turned as weak as a kitten's at the lascivious look in his eyes. As much as it thrilled her to have him want her so, Grace definitely sensed a need to put a little breathing space before the answering leap of desire that he inevitably ignited. Right now events seemed to be gathering speed with dizzying effect, and it would surely be wise to take some time out to reflect upon where they might be leading her. *She had a powerful notion that they were going to lead to the breaking of her heart.*

The thought of not seeing Marco again when the time came for them to part was frighteningly distressing—but he was a rich and influential man who had brief flings like this with women all the time. Now Grace's stomach really *did* plummet. She hated the idea of him making love to any other woman but *her*. When she'd seen the stylish and picture-perfect Francesca Bellini it had been hard not to feel a little insecure. She might have fooled herself that she would take a 'wait and see' approach to the possibility that Marco might have made her pregnant, but in truth her feelings were not remotely so *laissez-faire*.

What would she do if she *was* carrying his baby? An answering frisson of excitement arrowed through her but, telling herself to get a grip, she quickly poured cold water on the feeling. Yes, she loved children, but she hadn't planned on becoming a mother herself until she was in a stable and loving relationship. Besides...men like Marco Aguilar didn't fall in love with girls like Grace, so the sooner she disabused herself of *that* ridiculous little notion, the better.

Anyway...her thoughts ran on...there was still so much she wanted to accomplish in her work with the charity. She definitely wanted to return to the African village to visit the wonderful children she'd befriended and see the new orphanage finally standing proud...maybe even a school too? The next time she visited she might even extend her stay and help teach some basic reading and writing skills herself.

Touching her palm to the side of Marco's clean-shaven face, she made her smile as nonchalant as she could. 'I trust what you're thinking is *We really should go shopping now, or else Grace will look slightly the worse for wear in the crumpled dress she's wearing for the second day running?*' she quipped.

Gathering her hand, Marco pressed his lips warmly into the centre of her palm. 'I confess my thoughts are more along the lines of *I really want to strip off that pretty dress of hers and take her back to bed.* Are you surprised?'

'Flattered, maybe...but not surprised, no.' With an apologetic shrug, she quickly stepped out of the circle of his arms. 'But I really would like to get some fresh clothes on soon. We don't have to go shopping. In fact it would be much easier if Miguel just drops me back at the villa and I choose something from my own wardrobe.'

'Uh-uh. You don't get out of it that easily. I want to show you Vilamoura Marina. There are plenty of very nice clothes shops there for you to browse in, as well as a good selection of restaurants and bars we can choose

from when we're ready to have lunch. So come…we'll
go and find Miguel and enjoy a leisurely drive there.'

Marco had never known a woman so reluctant to shop.
Grace had already told him that shopping was never
going to be on her list of priorities, but he'd hoped that
when she learned money was no object and he would
gladly buy her anything she wanted she would change
her mind. That wasn't the case. She made some polite
comments here and there regarding the clothes or jewellery that he steered her towards, in the hope of getting an
interested response, but on the whole seemed singularly
unimpressed. His frustration grew—would she allow
him to buy her anything at all?

Then, half an hour into their tour of the stunning
marina, with its plethora of expensive yachts lining the
harbour and exclusive boutiques, he noticed that they'd
acquired the inevitable entourage—consisting of inquisitive sightseers plus a good few of the locals who had
recognised him. His sense of protectiveness towards
Grace strengthened even more. When she too realised
they were being followed he sensed her uneasiness, and
Marco knew her mind was far away from the meant-to-
be enjoyable task of choosing a new dress.

Feeling increasingly irritated, he firmly held onto his
companion's small hand as they stopped in front of one
of the most reputable and expensive boutiques on the
marina. Glancing round to face the small knot of locals
and holidaymakers that trailed them, he sighed and said,
'Come on, guys. I'm trying to enjoy a rare day off, here.
Don't you enjoy doing the same with your families and
friends? Leave us in peace and go about your business.
I promise you there are far more interesting sights to see

on the marina than me trying to impress my beautiful companion.'

An agreeable cheer went up, followed by a couple of risqué comments made by two young men at the back.

'Is she your new girlfriend, Marco? We all thought your preference was for brunettes.' This even bolder remark emanated from a lanky Australian in Hawaiian-style shorts and a baggy yellow T-shirt, who had positioned himself at the front of the onlookers. As he spoke, he was busily snapping shot after shot of Marco and Grace with a professional-looking camera.

Recognising the man as a regular member of the paparazzi that showed up at various functions and events he attended, Marco drew in a deep breath. 'I think you've taken enough pictures, and I'd like you to stop. As far as my preference about anything goes, the truth is that you don't know me well enough to have an opinion.'

He'd stupidly kidded himself that he could get away with just strolling round the marina with Grace and nothing untoward would bother them. He'd even given his bodyguard José strict instructions to wait by the car and not follow them. Today he'd just wanted to be like any other man holidaying with his wife or girlfriend. It seemed the perhaps *foolish* hope he'd secretly nurtured was to be denied.

Glancing at Grace, he pulled her firmly into his side.

'We don't have to do this today,' she murmured, her cornflower-blue eyes utterly bewitching as she glanced up at him from beneath sweeping fair lashes. 'We can shop another day.'

'No!' he snapped. 'That is *not* what I want. What I want is to buy you a dress, and I want to do it today. Come with me.'

He herded her ahead of him through the shop's glitzy

glass and gold entrance and when the pencil-slim brunette with silver flashes in her hair standing behind the
marble kidney-shaped counter, came over straight away
to attend them Marco didn't waste time with preliminar-
ies. The woman had immediately recognised him, he saw,
and that was all to the good.

'Close the shop,' he briskly instructed her in
Portuguese, nodding towards the small knot of onlookers with their cameras that stood outside—still determinedly taking pictures despite his plea. 'As you can see,
senhora, I have an unwanted entourage. Don't worry—if
you close the shop I will compensate you for any loss of
custom.'

'It will be my pleasure to do as you ask, Senhor
Aguilar.' Briefly turning away, the woman called out
for assistance.

Within seconds, a thickset young man with cropped
brown hair, dressed in a security guard's uniform appeared. Judging by the nicks and scars on both his face
and his hands, it looked as if his chosen sport was bare-
knuckle fighting, Marco observed wryly. Following a
very brief exchange with the woman—presumably his
boss—he immediately stepped outside and shut the heavy
glass door behind him. Marco felt a little more able to
relax when he saw the man firmly plant his feet and fold
his arms across his ample chest—his intimidating stance
alone transmitted a warning to anyone that dared to try
and get passed him.

'When you are ready to leave we have an exit at the
back.' The woman whose silver-grey badge on her lapel
proclaimed her name as Natalie gave him an unreserved
broad smile.

'That's good to know. Thank you.' He turned his
glance back to Grace. Some of the rosiness in her cheeks

had definitely faded, he saw. He had a feeling that she
was really hating what he'd hoped would turn out to be
a nice experience. 'Are you okay?' he asked, and it was
hard to keep the strain from his voice.

'I'm fine. I'm more concerned about you. You must
really get fed up with all this intrusive attention.'

'Some days it definitely bothers me more than others,
but I refuse to let anyone spoil our time together. We've
come to one of the most exclusive boutiques on the marina, so we ought to buy you a dress, no? I am sure that
Natalie here will give you all the assistance you need to
help you choose.'

Grace spun round on her heel to observe warily the
very select display of women's clothing that hung on
wafer-thin mannequins. 'There probably isn't anything
here above a size zero. Don't you think that's an insane
concept? Are all the women in the world trying to dis-
appear?'

'Go and have a proper look,' Marco urged, his hand
lightly touching her back.

Silently he agreed with her. The attentive and perfectly made-up Natalie transmitted a sympathetic look
to him that immediately rubbed him up the wrong way.
Having already seen her arrow a glance straight in on
Grace's slightly rumpled red and white dress, and fail to
hide her distaste, he abhorred the idea that the woman
believed for even a second that she was somehow *better*
than his lovely, unaffected companion.

'Why don't you show her what you have?' he said
tersely. 'Presumably that's what you are being paid for,
Natalie?'

'Of course, Senhor Aguilar… May I ask what the
young lady's name is?'

'I'm sure you can manage just fine without it.'

'Of course.' The uneasy smile she gave him was visibly nervous.

'And when my friend finds something that she likes, I would like to see her wearing it.'

'Yes, *senhor.*'

Natalie dipped her head in a short, respectful bow, and when she moved across the room to join Grace he registered with relief that her tone was far more helpful. His tension easing a little, Marco strolled across the marble floor to one of several white couches dotted round. Dropping down into one, he reached for the neatly folded newspaper that lay on the table in front of him.

Feeling uncomfortably pressured to choose a dress that she hadn't even wanted in the first place, but at the same time wanting to please Marco and not add to the palpable tension she sensed in him, Grace took the strapless smocked dress she'd finally selected, which they thankfully had in her size, and went into the scented and luxurious changing room to try it on. When Natalie offered to come in and help her she straight away called out that she could manage just fine by herself. She'd bet her last penny that the older woman was busy wondering what a man like Marco must see in a very average sort of girl like her.

Especially when he preferred brunettes...

Unhappily she recalled the Australian photographer's tactless jibe, and consequently derived no pleasure in trying on the pretty and feminine maxi-dress whose attached labels were festooned with a French designer's name all over them. She was more than discomfited to discover there was no price-tag in evidence. And even though the changing room was more than adequately air-conditioned, Grace was suddenly too hot, not to mention feeling a little claustrophobic after being stalked by that intrusive little crowd waiting for them outside.

How did Marco bear it? From what she knew of him he didn't seem like a man who craved the constant attention of admirers *or* the press. He was essentially a very private man. She had a real yearning to be alone with him again, to ascertain if he really *was* doing all right, and to tell him that she would much prefer to spend the rest of her time with him talking and relaxing rather than going out, with him misguidedly feeling as if he needed to buy her things to keep her happy. Hadn't he learned enough of her nature to know that that would *never* be the case where she was concerned?

Her fingers fumbling with the lavender-coloured ribbon on the ruched bodice of the dress, she almost jumped out of her skin when her mobile phone's salsa beat ringtone broke into her reverie. Dropping down to the carpeted floor to delve inside her straw bag, she located the phone, fully expecting the call to be from her parents. She hadn't spoken to them in over three days now, and no doubt they were getting anxious about her.

But the number that was flashing didn't belong to her mum or dad. It belonged to Sarah, the manager of the children's charity in London. Grace frowned, her heart bumping in alarm.

By the time the conversation came to an end she was sitting on the floor, leaning against the changing room wall, with her knees drawn up to her chest and scalding tears of grief and aching regret streaking down her face. Someone knocked on the door. When she didn't respond, it was immediately pushed open. *It was Marco.*

'The manager told me that she heard you crying. What has happened? Are you hurt?' Suddenly his handsome face was right in front of hers as he dropped down to the same level as Grace, his fingers concernedly squeezing her shoulder.

'I've had some bad news.' She sniffed, hastily wiping her eyes. At the same time she registered that she was probably creasing a very expensive designer dress that Marco would have to pay for. The panicked thought added to the drowning sensation of sorrow and distress that was already washing over her, breaking her heart.

'Somebody rang you from home?' Lifting her hand, Marco examined the slim silver mobile she was still gripping. 'Tell me what's wrong, I beg you. I cannot bear seeing you so upset and not knowing the reason.'

Grace lifted her sorrowful gaze to meet his, striving with all her might to gain better control over her emotions and utterly failing. 'Remember the baby I told you about back in Africa?'

'Azizi you said his name was?'

She was startled that he should recall that.

'Yes. I remember. You told me that it meant beloved or precious one.' The hooded dark eyes in front of her had deepened to almost black.

'Well...my manager just phoned to tell me that he—that he *died*. A couple of days ago he developed a fever, and although one of the charity workers managed to get him to a hospital in the city he had a bad fit during the night and—and he didn't make it. He was just a few weeks old...' Pausing to wipe away another tear, Grace had tremendous difficulty in swallowing across the aching lump inside her throat. 'It doesn't seem fair does it? I mean...to have had such a tragic start in life and then to die just as tragically before you'd even had the chance to live. You said that Azizi would be fortunate if he lived up to his name...now he *won't*...'

'*Não chorar, a meu amor, que o bebê e seguro com*

Deus agora.' The words were out before Marco had re-alised he would say them out loud. It literally made his heart ache to see Grace like this and the need to console her took precedence over everything else…even the risk of his words being overheard by the woman who ran the boutique and reported back to the press for a no doubt ludicrous sum…

The shimmering blue eyes in front of him widened as his hand tenderly stroked back her hair, then cupped her cheek. 'What does that mean?' she asked, her voice lowered to a mesmerised whisper.

'I said, do not cry any more. The baby is safe with God now.' *He didn't even know if he believed in God.* Perhaps his early programming of being raised as a Catholic in the orphanage had made him err towards believing rather than not—even though some people might regard his own start in life as tragic and not understand it. He omitted to tell Grace that he'd actually said, 'Do not cry any more, *my love'*. Never in his life had Marco addressed a woman in such a tender way. It jolted him to realise what a dif-ferent man he was around her.

'That's beautiful. Thank you.'

'I will do everything I can to help you come to terms with this loss, Grace…I promise. Would you prefer to go home and have lunch rather than eat here at the marina?'

She looked relieved. 'Can we? I'm really sorry… I didn't mean to spoil your plans for the day.'

His throat a little tight, Marco forced a smile. 'You have spoiled nothing, my angel.'

Helping her to her feet, he felt his senses suddenly be-sieged by her—by the exquisite softness of the hands he held onto—almost as if she were a lifeline, helping him out of the sea of loneliness and pain that had dogged his footsteps ever since he was a child. No matter how much worldly success he'd achieved. Knowing he was staring, he was staggered by the natural beauty and grace that seemed to define her so effortlessly... *Grace* was the perfect name for her. *How had her parents known that their daughter would grow up to embody it?*

'Marco? Don't you like the dress?'

He gazed at her, unable to look away. The beautiful garment she wore with its riot of spring colours was lovely. But more than the dress itself, it was the bewitching girl who wore it that elevated it to something special. Caught up in the spell of her, the ability to respond with mere words deserted him.

'Marco? What's wrong? You're worrying me.'

Gathering her urgently into his arms, he crushed her to him and kissed her as if he might *die* if he didn't.

Neither he nor Grace heard the changing room door open and Natalie murmur, '*Desculpe me*...excuse me...' then quietly and discreetly leave.

CHAPTER TEN

TRUE to her word, Natalie had shown them out the back way, and thankfully they'd escaped the notice of the predatory crowd waiting for them to emerge outside the front of the boutique. They'd run all the way back to the car, and had both been breathless when they arrived. Miguel had given them a bemused glance, then gunned the engine, and they'd left the glamorous marina behind to travel back to the villa.

Marco held her hand throughout the entire journey. Grace fought hard to contain her grief—lodged like a burning stone inside her chest as she recalled gazing down into Azizi's big brown eyes and seeing the absolute trust there that she would take care of him. She had had a special bond with the baby boy since the night a co-worker had put him into her arms. At every opportunity she had held him, bathed him, sung to him if he was fractious and it cut like a knife that she would never take care of him again...

Stealing into the midst of her grief came the thought that she might have a baby of her own if Marco had made her pregnant. Instead of making her feel apprehensive, as it had done before, the idea actually started to console her. She even began to pray that it would come true. Even though he'd said that he didn't have any good ex-

ample of what it meant to be a father, Grace didn't doubt
that Marco would make a good one. She'd had too many
examples of his kindness and concern for people *not* to
believe it. If he could only endeavour not to keep his emotions locked up so tightly they might even have a future
together, she mused.

The notion rocked her world off its axis.

Lifting her gaze to his as the car drew nearer to the
villa, she became intimately aware of the hungrily burning intensity that glowed in her companion's hooded dark
eyes. It caught her in a spell that even the most powerful
magic would never free her from. It was as though every
unfulfilled hope, dream and desire they'd ever had had
erupted inside them the moment his lips had brushed hers
in the changing room back at the boutique. It had literally
been like touching flame to tinder. And now they were
set on a course to fulfil those dreams and desires…

As soon as they'd reached the villa and gone in, Marco
waited only until they were at the foot of the grand stair-
case before sweeping Grace off her feet into his arms and
transporting her upstairs to the bedroom. Once there,
they hungrily tore at each other's clothes, sharing each
other's breath with drugging, rapturous kisses, until they
fell onto the bed in a flurry of searching hands and tan-
gled limbs, eager and impatient to stop the world and any
notion of pain or sadness—to make love until they were
utterly spent and exhausted.

Lying on her front in the opulent bed, the covers in a
pool of oyster silk around her, Grace turned her head to
examine the lazily sexy smile of the man beside her. 'Do
you have any idea how much I like you, Marco Aguilar?'
she whispered.

Exhaling a long, slow breath, he trailed his fingertips
up and down her spine, sending a cascade of delicious

shivers throughout her body. 'Why don't you tell me?' he urged.

'I like you more than any other man I've ever met… But please don't let that scare you. It doesn't mean I expect any more than you've already given me or are willing to give while we're together.'

'Why do you think it would scare me to hear you say that?' His ebony brows lifted quizzically.

'Because I get the feeling you don't want anyone to get too attached…especially a woman.'

'You think so?'

'Why don't you answer the question? *Do* you fear a woman getting too close to you, Marco?'

His fingers stopped trailing up and down her spine. His expression had a shuttered look about it, and Grace tensed apprehensively.

'What do you think?' he said slowly. 'Everyone that should have been close to me…would have been close to me…I've lost. Maybe I associate becoming too attached to someone with loss? Can you wonder why I wouldn't want it?'

Even though she knew he was reluctant to talk about personal things, Grace sensed a definite opening in his usual guard—perhaps brought about by their passionate and tender lovemaking? She hoped so. At any rate, she wouldn't let the possibility of a deeper conversation go.

'Marco…?'

'Hmm?'

Reaching out, he manoeuvred her round into his arms, smiling wickedly and making her heart race like mad. Poignantly, she saw how he hoped to deflect her questions with humour.

'What is it now, my angel? Think of me as your very own personal genie…your wish is my command.'

She sucked in a breath. 'Will you talk to me…? I mean *really* talk to me?'

If her request disturbed him, there was no immediate indication that it did.

'What is it that you want to discuss? Tell me.'

'I'd like to talk about *you…*'

'Ah.'

'You just mentioned the loss in your life. Can I ask you about your childhood?'

'What do you want to know about it?'

'You said that your father abandoned you in the orphanage when your mother died? Did you ever find out where he went afterwards? I mean, did he never get in touch with you while you were there?'

The sudden tension in his muscles was slight, but she immediately detected it and held her breath.

'The answer is no to both questions. My mother and father were sixteen and seventeen respectively. They were both orphans…no parents, no home. When my mother died giving birth to me my father was apparently so broken-hearted that all he could think of to do when he went back to the hospital to collect me was take me to the orphanage where he himself had been raised—in fact where he and my mother had met. At the time he was doing some casual labour to make money, and was renting a small inadequate room in the town. He pleaded with them to take me because he had neither the means nor the ability to raise me by himself…and no doubt that was true. After promising to keep in contact, he left. They never saw him again.'

Rubbing his hand across his eyes, Marco deliberately averted his gaze.

'It's not easy to find a seventeen-year-old youth with

no forwarding address, and no family through which he might be traced either.'

Carefully, gently, Grace flattened her palm against his chest. His heartbeat was racing slightly, and he took a long breath in, then slowly blew it out again. She waited for a few moments for him to start talking again. When he didn't, she rested her head where her hand had been. His breathing was steadier now, and his hard-muscled chest with its dusting of soft dark hair was warm and wonderful to lie against...like the safest haven she could imagine. Despite his sad upbringing he had such tenacity. She marvelled at the psychological strength it must have taken to rise above the painful start he'd had in life and—against all the odds—achieve something as remarkable as without a doubt he had.

'Your parents would have been so proud of you if they'd seen you grow up,' she murmured, tears filling her eyes not only for Marco, but for Azizi too—a boy that had also never known his parents. It was hard to understand why life had to be so hard and cruel sometimes.

'Hey.' Marco moved back so that he could study her. 'Are you crying for me? If you are, then don't. I don't want you shedding tears for what happened a long time ago...*too* long. My own policy is never to look back. I've put it all behind me now and I have no regrets.'

Grace cupped his beard-shadowed jaw. 'I'm crying for you *and* for Azizi. Childhood is so precious. Is it true, Marco? Is it true that you don't ever think about yours and wish things might have been different?'

His gaze was completely unwavering as he considered her, and the sun streamed through the huge windows, illuminating the tiny flecks of light in his dark pupils. 'Yes, it's true. I never think about the past and wish it had been different. What on earth would be the point?'

'Were you ever happy at all when you were growing up in the orphanage?'

'Not particularly, no. Are your orphans in Africa happy?'

'Sometimes they are. Their lives are challenging, of course. But they take one day at a time... Children live in the moment, don't they? They don't occupy themselves in regretting the past and fretting about the future. And if an adult is kind to them, pays them attention and gives them a hug, their smiles are unbelievable. They respond with so much love that it takes your breath away. It's the most rewarding work...helping to make them happy even for just a little while.'

'It must be for someone like *you*, Grace.'

'Like I told you before...I'm not the only one who loves those kids. You would love them too if you met them. Wasn't there *anyone* who looked after you when you were little that loved you, and you loved back?'

Scowling, he sat up, dragging the covers over his knees. 'Not that I recall. Are we finished talking about me now? I think we are, because I can tell you I've had enough of revisiting the past for one day and I'd like you to respect that.'

'I'm really sorry if it distresses you to talk about such things. but—'

'No doubt you think it's for my own good?' His ensuing sigh was heavy, and laden with irritation. 'You think it might help me release some of the hurt of rejection you imagine I feel inside and make me feel better about myself, is that it? *Deus!* You are like a dog with a bone when you want to get to the bottom of things aren't you, Grace?'

'I only want to try and help.'

'Well, don't. I'm not one of the coterie of orphans

you're intent on saving single-handedly. The only way you can help me is by being the companion I want you to be for the duration of this holiday and by sharing my bed—*not* by being a latter-day Mother Teresa! If I need to explore any angst about the past I'll go to a psychologist.'

For long moments his furious tirade crushed her. Then Grace determinedly called upon the reservoir of strength she always drew from whenever she had a challenge to face. She stowed away her embarrassment at being so brutally put in her place and somehow found a smile. Something told her that Marco's anger wasn't about her encroaching upon his painful memories of the past, but purely because he was furious with himself that those memories still haunted him.

'I hear you. Again, I'm really sorry if I've made you feel uncomfortable in any way. Let's talk about something else, shall we?'

Driving his fingers roughly through his burnished dark hair, he stared at her hard. 'Good idea. How about we talk about *you* instead, hmm? For instance, who was the guy you lost your virginity to? Let's start with that, shall we?'

She'd risked upsetting Marco and now she was paying the price. However, believing as she did that talking was good, she wouldn't flinch from telling him what he wanted to know. Perhaps her own story would help defuse his anger and frustration with himself?

Sitting up beside him, Grace turned her head to directly meet his gaze. 'He was just a guy I briefly dated at university. We only slept together that one time. It was hardly love's young dream—just the opposite, in fact. Because in the morning he told me he'd made a mistake…

that he preferred someone else but hadn't been able to bring himself to tell me.'

'So he stole your virginity just for the hell of it, then went on to some other poor, gullible woman?'

Shrugging, she folded her arms round her knees. 'We both made a mistake. I'm not proud of it. You do some stupid things when you're young—especially when you're looking for acceptance and approval.'

Sliding his hand round her jaw, Marco made her turn her head so that he could intimately examine her face. 'You're too hard on yourself. It's the guy who was stupid...stupid to think there was someone better than you.'

'Thanks,' she murmured, hoping and praying that the tenderness she heard in his voice meant he wouldn't stay mad at her for long, for daring to quiz him about his past.

'And what about the guy that assaulted you?' he asked gently. 'What was your relationship like with him?'

Her insides knotting, Grace grimaced. 'It wasn't anything special, if that's what you're asking. We just kind of fell into going out with each other because we enjoyed the same kind of movies and music... For a while he'd been a part of the group of friends I hung out with, so when he asked me out I believed I knew him—I thought he'd be okay...that he'd treat me well. Everything was fine until he started pressing me to sleep with him. I kept resisting, because I didn't even know if I liked him enough to keep on dating him, let alone have an intimate relationship. We went to a party one night. He'd been drinking steadily throughout the evening so I drove us home. He didn't want to be dropped off at his place, and asked if we could go back to mine for a cup of coffee, saying he would ring a cab to take him home. I agreed. It was a stupid decision, because at the time I really believed that was all he wanted. But as soon as we got inside my flat he started accusing me of flirting with some guy at the party. It wasn't true…not *remotely*. Anyway, he started shoving me around a bit, then he pinned me to the floor and—'

She couldn't continue. The memory made Grace feel sick and wretched, scared too that she seemed to be so hopeless at choosing the right men.

'I shouldn't have made you talk about it…I'm sorry'

Easing her head down onto his chest, Marco threaded his long fingers through her tousled fair hair and tenderly massaged her scalp. It had been despicable of him to make her recall the man who had hurt her, but his own anger and pain about the past—and jealousy too, at the idea of Grace being with anyone else before him—had made him temporarily and regrettably cruel.

She shifted, and a soft sigh feathered over the surface of his skin, raining him with goose bumps. 'I don't mind you asking me about my previous relationships… if that's what you could even call them. When you're intimate with someone it's only natural that you want to know as much as you can about them.' Moving to sit up next to him, she shook back her prettily mussed blonde hair and folded her arms. 'When we first met you asked me if I had a boyfriend and I said no. You never told me if *you* had anyone on the scene. Is there? Is there some woman somewhere that you care about, Marco? Someone you maybe should have mentioned to me?'

Staring up at the ornate ceiling, he momentarily rested his forearm against his brow. Reflecting on the abhorrent treatment he'd received from his ex-girlfriend Jasmine, when she'd had the audacity to take him to court for breach of his so-called promise to support her when she'd been fired from her job, he scowled.

'No. Of course there's no one else. I wouldn't do that

to you—ask you to spend your holiday with me and share my bed if there was another woman on the scene. I know plenty of rich men that play the field...but I'm not one of them.'

'That's good to know' she replied softly, with the full force of her bewitching blue glance coming to rest unwaveringly on his face. 'Can you perhaps tell me what your last girlfriend was like? Could you at least share that with me?'

He laughed harshly, then sat up. 'If you really want to know, she was a total nightmare! I was well rid of her in the end.'

'What happened?'

'Nothing that I care to revisit or talk about.'

Grace had that look on her face that told Marco she wasn't going to let him off the hook so lightly, and inside he knew he would have to concede.

'But I just told you about *my* previous relationships... even though it was painful.'

'Okay.' He held up his hands in an exaggerated gesture of surrender, then raked his fingers through his already mussed hair. 'She was a fashion model whose looks I was briefly and foolishly enamoured with. I should have looked a lot deeper than the surface package she presented, but for some reason I didn't. Perhaps I was lonely at the time? Who knows?' He snorted disparagingly. 'It turned out that she was addicted not just to very rich and gullible men but to cocaine—and any number of other addictive drugs too. When the fashion house she worked for didn't renew her contract, because frankly she was becoming a liability, she took me to court claiming I'd promised to support her. I did no such thing. I had told her we were finished even before she lost her damn job!'

'That must have hurt…to have a woman you cared for betray you like that,' Grace murmured sympathetically.

His eyes narrowed. 'I didn't say that I cared for her.'

'It still must have hurt.'

Relenting, Marco caught hold of her hand. 'It was my pride that was hurt more than anything else. But why are we even talking about this? Can't we just forget about our pasts and concentrate on what's going on right now? I have a suggestion. Why don't you put on that pretty new dress and we'll go out?'

'Out where?'

'We'll drive to my yacht and take a cruise round the bay.'

'You have a *yacht*?'

'What self-respecting billionaire doesn't?' he joked, his breathtaking smile dazzling her. 'I only have to make a call and the crew will make it ready for us. What kind of food would you like to eat? I can phone one of many restaurants and get them to deliver our order to the yacht. We can sit on the deck and eat out under the stars.'

Grace sighed. She saw how the idea of going to his yacht and arranging for their dinner to be delivered from a fine restaurant immediately put Marco back in control, returning him to the world of elite lifestyles that he'd grown comfortable with…where he knew who he was and what he wanted…where he could merely snap his fingers and have a bevy of eager retainers hurry to do his will. It also helped him temporarily hide from the hurt of his childhood, when he patently *hadn't* been in control of what happened to him.

But he couldn't hide from it for ever. That would make for a very hard and unhappy existence, no matter *how* much money he had, Grace thought. Sooner or later everyone had to face the truth of their lives.

She'd already personally learned that repeating the same patterns—going down old familiar roads where nothing challenged you any more—didn't help ease or heal anything. It just brought more of the same silent despair that day by day ate away at your soul. *Unless you turned and faced it, that was.* That was why she'd gone out to Africa. At the time she'd been so scared of what she might encounter when she'd flown out there—the suffering she would undoubtedly see and have to find a way of dealing with—that she'd thought she would be more of a hindrance than a help. What Grace hadn't been prepared for was the joy and satisfaction she'd experienced at having the trusting sweet smile of a previously distressed or despairing child turned on *her*. The very things she'd feared had turned out to be her salvation.

Carefully disengaging her hand from Marco's, she registered the flicker of unease that crossed his glance. 'As lovely as that sounds, I'm afraid I'm going to have to say no. In fact I'm going to ask instead if I can have a little time to myself. There are a few things I need to think about.'

'You mean like the baby dying?'

'Yes.'

'I know he didn't live for long, but he was a lucky boy to have someone like you looking after him Grace...even for a little while. You asked me if I ever thought about the past...if I'd ever loved anyone that had helped to take care of me. If I had had someone like you, I would have thought myself blessed beyond measure, believe me.'

A hopeful breath shuddered through her. 'You deserved to have the very best of care and attention, Marco...*and* love. It breaks my heart to think that you didn't.'

He said nothing for a while, but his tension of earlier

had palpably eased. Then he considered her thoughtfully and said, 'You came to the Algarve for a rest and a break from work…to *enjoy* yourself. Let's go out to the yacht together. I guarantee you will not regret it.'

It hurt Grace to deny him anything…especially in light of his previous confession about his childhood. To do so made her feel as if she was another adult who had let him down. That was hard to bear, when she knew that she loved him with all her heart.

The realisation made her catch her breath. She wanted to laugh and cry at the same time. *She was in love.* She was completely and totally head over heels.

It became even more imperative that she have some time to herself—to absorb this stunning revelation, to reflect and consider what to do next.

'I'm sorry, Marco. I really just need to be by myself for a while. Please try and understand.'

'Okay. Selfishly, it's not what I want…to let you go for even an *hour* let alone an entire evening feels indescribably hard…but I see that you need time to come to terms with the baby's death by yourself, so I won't try to stop you from going.'

Grace made herself breathe deeply. 'Thanks for that. It's only for this one evening. I promise I'll come back in the morning—if you don't mind asking Miguel to pick me up?'

'Of course I don't mind. You might also bring a suitcase with some of your clothes in it when you return. It makes sense for you to stay here for the remainder of your holiday, don't you think?'

'I suppose it does. Well, then… I'd better get dressed.' Moving to the edge of the bed, Grace tugged at one of the silk covers and wrapped it round her bare form, deliberately taking her time and not hurrying, in case Marco mistakenly believed she was eager to get away.

The words 'for the remainder of your holiday' rang anxiously in her ears, confirming that he clearly didn't believe they could have a future together.

On leaden legs she moved quietly round the room, bit by bit gathering her scattered clothing as memories of the afternoon's passionate lovemaking deluged her, making her want to run straight back to him and beg him to love her again…to confess that she loved him.

Having not the slightest clue as to how he might receive such a confession, she knew it made even more sense that she have some time on her own to mull things over.

Registering the sound of his moving behind her, Grace glanced over her shoulder to see him pulling on his chinos, his expression grim, absorbed in the private landscape of his thoughts. Then he scraped his fingers through the dark strands of hair that she loved so much to touch and turning to face her, exhaled deeply.

'Although I've agreed to let you go, I hate the thought of you being upset tonight and my not being there to help comfort you.'

The confession really touched her. 'I'll think about you saying that and just the thought will help comfort me, Marco. It's only for this one evening, remember? The time will soon go. What will you do? Will you go out to your yacht as planned?'

'Probably not. I think I'll go and catch up with some friends of mine for the evening instead. I'm not often in the country, so I guess it would be a good opportunity.'

'I agree. That sounds like a good idea. Your friends must miss not seeing you, Marco.'

He didn't respond. Instead he pulled his still buttoned

white shirt over his head, slipped his bare feet into tan loafers and moved across the vast expanse of marble flooring to the door.

'Help yourself to a shower before you leave,' he said over his shoulder, 'I'll go and find Miguel to tell him I want him to drive you home. When you're ready, just go and find him at the front of the house…he'll be waiting for you there. I'll also arrange for him to pick you up in the morning.'

'Thanks…' Her heart was beating double-time because he suddenly sounded so distant and businesslike. He plainly wasn't going to kiss her goodbye either. Was it a mistake to insist that she needed some time to herself this evening? Grace prayed that it wasn't…

CHAPTER ELEVEN

THE inconsequential chatter of the people sitting with him round the restaurant table washed over Marco—as though the voices came from far away...as if he was locked inside a dream. Because Grace wasn't with him, the evening was quickly taking on the quality of a nightmare. The two of them had only been apart for a few short hours, but already it felt like an eternity. There was a dull ache inside his chest, his appetite had completely disappeared, and he could hardly summon up the energy or interest to talk to his friends.

Friends... The word seemed to mock him as he glanced round at the faces of colleagues past and present. Why were all his so-called friendships work-related? he pondered. The reason he'd agreed to accept the invitation to join them tonight and had scrapped his intention to go to his yacht was because he hadn't wanted to be alone with his thoughts. He hadn't wanted to be alone, *per se*. Yet it hardly helped that the people at dinner weren't *real* friends at all.

Marco reflected that no doubt his driven desire to be a success had severed any possibility of making genuine friends from all walks of life, instead of just the elite he'd worked so hard to join. The chances had simply passed him by because his focus had been too pointed to notice them. It didn't help that most of his time was spent either *at* work, embroiled in some lengthy boardroom meeting, making deals with equally driven businessmen or women over lunch or dinner, or *thinking* about work in some way—even when he was meant to be relaxing, playing golf, or when he was at some glitzy party or casino.

Apart from working and pleasure-seeking, what else had he done with his life? Yes, he supported several different charities by donating money and being a patron, but when had he ever put himself out to get more personally involved, like Grace did? *What was he so afraid of?*

The answer came to Marco without any effort at all. Because he'd lived in what might be deemed an ivory tower for so long, he harboured a secret fear of exposing himself as hopeless when it came to everyday interactions with ordinary people. More than that, he feared he might have to face the fact that being so emotionally shut down was depriving him of some real joy and satisfaction in his life. The kind that came from really connecting with people and helping them make their lives better.

Marco's painfully analytical stream of thought didn't exactly help him feel any better about the situation—even though he knew he needed to take a good hard look at these things. The only thing that had the remotest chance of improving his mood right now was seeing Grace. *He had so easily let her go.* Why hadn't he argued more emphatically for her to stay? He hadn't even kissed her goodbye.

The arresting image of her standing in his bedroom with nothing but a silk sheet wrapped round her, to cover her shapely naked form, sent such a surge of longing pulsing through him that he briefly shut his eyes to contain it.

What if he never saw her again? What if she concluded in their time apart this evening that he was too shut-down for her to get close to? Too removed from the so-called 'real world' for her ever to reach?

Reaching for his wine glass, he was so deep in thought that he accidentally knocked it over with the heel of his hand, sending a wave of cranberry coloured liquid flying over the pristine white tablecloth. The two glamorous women sitting on either side of him jumped up in dismay—anxious not to get wine on their expensive outfits, but also quick to reassure him that accidents could happen to anyone.

Marco had risen to his feet at the same time, grabbing a white linen napkin to mop up the spill, uncaring that some of it splashed the sleeve of his exclusive Armani suit. Seconds later a helpful waiter attended to the mopping up much more efficiently, and with the minimum of fuss. That was the moment when Marco made the decision to quit the party. The hot, prickling sensation of feeling hemmed in and trapped had started to creep up on him again, and he desperately craved some fresh air.

Making his apologies, he accepted the generous offer from one of his colleagues to pay his share of the bill, wished everyone goodnight, and walked as if in a dream slowly down the restaurant's lantern-lit walkway to the car.

'Miguel?' When they arrived back home Marco paused as he got out of the car.

'Yes, *senhor*?'

'Join me for a drink?'

With a mute nod, Marco's loyal chauffeur followed him back inside the villa. The two men strolled out onto one of the myriad balconies that decked the building, but not before Marco had stopped by the wine cellar in the basement and collected a bottle of vintage red wine and a couple of glasses on the way. Throwing his jacket with the stained sleeve onto a nearby wrought-iron bench, he pulled out a chair from the matching table and gestured to the other man to do likewise.

Taking his time to pour the wine carefully, he gave a glass to Miguel, then made a toast. 'To truth and beauty.'

With a contemplative smile, the chauffeur touched his glass to Marco's and silently concurred. They sat companionably for a while, with just the shrill sound of the cicadas interrupting the tranquil silence that fell around them. *It was peaceful.* It made Marco realise just how much he valued the steady, thoughtful presence of the other man.

'You miss her.'

'Excuse me?'

'Senhorita Faulkner…you miss her'

Marco shook his head in wonder that his employee should intuit so much. 'We have only been apart for one evening,' he said ruefully.

'It makes no difference.' Miguel shrugged a shoulder. 'When the most important woman in your life is lost to you even briefly it feels like you will never be whole again until you see her.'

'What makes you think that Senhorita Faulkner is the most important woman in my life? She is *not*. How could she be when I have only known her for the shortest time?'

Even as he rushed to deny his true feelings—so soon after drinking a toast to 'truth and beauty'—Marco's heart raced with longing to be with Grace, to gaze into her lovely blue eyes, bring her lush sweet body close to his and know that everything was right in his world because he was with her.

'You can meet the woman of your dreams and fall in love with her in an instant. It does not matter that you have only just met her.' The chauffeur's gaze was unwavering and direct.

'How did you get to be so wise about affairs of the heart, my friend? Is that what happened to you?'

There was a distant look in Miguel's dark eyes that told Marco he was remembering someone who had meant a great deal to him once upon a time. Knowing that the man was now single, he was genuinely sorry that they'd never had a conversation personal enough for him to enquire about the relationships that had been meaningful to him.

'Yes…that is what happened to me.' Pausing to curl his hand round the stem of his wine glass, Miguel raised it thoughtfully to his lips and took a sip of the blood-red vintage. 'But sadly I lost the love of my life when she fell ill and what afflicted her turned out to be terminal. We only had the shortest time together, but it was intense and amazing, you know?'

Marco *did* know. 'I'm so sorry that you lost her,' he murmured consolingly.

Swallowing hard, Miguel shook off the anguish that must have shuddered through him and smiled. 'That is why you must make the most of the time you have with Senhorita Faulkner. I only have to see the way the two of you look at each other to know that you are in love.'

Even though it made him inwardly reel to hear the other man's statement, Marco had to own privately that for *his* part at least it was the truth. Did he dare believe that Grace might feel the same?

'Senhorita Faulkner…*Grace*…is an incredible

woman—warm-hearted and brave. I am a poor bargain for someone like her, Miguel,' he remarked soberly.

'I do not think so.'

'She's not impressed with who I am in the world, what I've achieved or how much money I have.'

'If that is so then you are a fortunate man indeed, *senhor*, because she must clearly desire you just for yourself.'

Two of the charity workers at the African orphanage had gone down with a fever similar to that which had afflicted Azizi and were in hospital. Grace had heard the news from her dad, when she'd rung home yesterday evening. A senior member of the charity who hadn't known Grace was in the Algarve had rung her parents' number in a bid to contact her.

As soon as her dad had revealed the news to her Grace had sensed his reluctance in passing it on, because he knew that she couldn't fail to act on it—perhaps to the detriment of her own health. Now there were only two full-time volunteers remaining at the orphanage to help take care of the children—a young man hired by the charity in London, that had arrived in Africa on the same day that she'd flown out, and a local grandmother and midwife. Running over the scenario again in her mind, imagining the distress of not only the two remaining volunteers at what had happened, but the children too, Grace didn't regret agreeing to fly out there at once to help.

But even in the midst of hearing about the worrying events back in Africa she'd been consumed with an uncontainable longing to be with Marco. *She shouldn't have left him.* Their difficult temporary parting—even though she had been the instigator of it—had left her feeling as if her heart had been cleaved in two, and she had spent a mostly miserable evening on her own, mulling over the fact that she was hopelessly in love with him and wondering how she was going to say goodbye and return to living without him?

The knock on the door as she drank her breakfast coffee propelled her already anxious thoughts into overdrive. On the way out of the living room into the hallway, she glanced over at the compact powder-blue suitcase standing by the couch. She'd originally hoped to pack it and take it with her back to Marco's. Now she would take it with her to a completely *different* destination.

Just before opening the door she paused to glance down at the knee-length aubergine-coloured dress she wore. She checked the back of the chignon her blonde hair had been fashioned into to make sure that the tortoiseshell clasp held it secure. She'd deliberately made an effort with her appearance in a bid to feel more confident when it came to facing Marco and telling him about her change of plans.

But the man she had been expecting to see standing on the other side of the door was his enigmatic chauffeur Miguel...*not* Marco himself, wearing a stylish fitted black shirt and jeans, his black hair swept back by his sunglasses to reveal his strong, indomitable forehead. His dark eyes instantly devoured her, making her legs feel dangerously weak and insubstantial. He resembled some gorgeous dark angel, come to tempt her into an erotic realm she'd never want to be free of so long as he was there, and Grace could hardly think straight, let alone string words together to greet him.

In the end it was he who spoke first. '*Deus!* You are looking especially beautiful this morning, Grace...elegant and sexy. I'm very glad that I came to pick you up myself rather than send Miguel.'

'Thanks...' she murmured, her cheeks glowing scarlet. She was torn between walking straight into his arms and

affecting enough distance between them so that the temptation wouldn't overwhelm her. 'It's good to see you…
really good. Why don't you come in? There's plenty of
coffee left in the cafetière…can you spare a few minutes
to have a cup with me?'

'Of course.'

Stepping inside, with a knowing little smile playing
round the corners of his lips because he'd sensed that she
was desperate to touch him, Marco glanced towards the
family photos that lined the hallway walls. They were
nearly all of Grace with her parents, at various stages of
her growing up. The latter ones were more recent shots
of her as an adult—at her graduation, and at the twenty-
first birthday party they'd thrown for her.

'I don't know why my parents want to have them all
on display.' Her dismissive shrug was helplessly self-
conscious, but Marco didn't immediately halt his examination of the pictures. In fact, he seemed more than a
little fascinated by them. An unhappy thought occurred
to Grace. Had anyone ever documented the phases of
his growing up? She wanted to weep at the notion that
they hadn't.

As the minutes ticked by, she became more and more
convinced that the idea that had taken hold of her last
night and wouldn't let go was a *good* one.

'They look like kind people…your parents, I mean.'

Turning round to face her, he folded his arms across
his chest and smiled…a little uncertainly, Grace reflected
with a pang. 'They are *very* kind. Shall we go through
onto the patio and have that coffee?'

The sunshine seemed especially glorious that morning, and the sky was a perfect duck-egg-blue. There was
a faint caressing breeze, and it carried the scent of bougainvillaea along with the smell of the suncream she'd

rubbed into her skin, making her wish that she could make the deceptively simple choice merely to enjoy this holiday—to have nothing else in her mind but to spend all her time with Marco.

'You take it black with no sugar, right?' she poured him some coffee and slid the porcelain cup on its saucer across the wooden table towards him. The crockery rattled a little, as if mimicking her nervousness.

Murmuring his thanks, he lowered his aviator sunglasses down over his eyes and instantly added to the mystique he exuded so effortlessly, making Grace's stomach take a slow elevator ride right down to the tips of her toes.

'I missed you last night,' she confessed softly, not looking away when his glance intensified.

'I missed you too, Grace.'

'So...how did you spend the evening? Did you go to see your friends?'

'Yes, I did... Although in truth they aren't really friends. Simply people I once worked with or still work with.'

'Oh?'

'There was a time when I would have referred to them as friends, but not any more.'

'Why's that?'

'Since spending time with you, Grace, I have begun to see more and more who I can count as real friends and who I cannot.'

His smile at her was slow as the most luxurious honey being poured over a waffle—and a thousand times more tempting.

'I've also faced up to the fact that I've been running away from my past instead of properly dealing with my feelings about it. Hearing you talk about your own fears, seeing how you've been determined to face them and overcome them, has made me see the sense in trying to do the same—because I don't want them to impinge any more on the present. You see what you've done to me? I am a changed man because of you.'

'I haven't done anything. If you've realised these things it's because you want to see the truth, Marco… that's all.' Grace absently stirred more sugar into her coffee, because being caught in the hypnotic beam of his disturbing gaze—even behind his shades—made it hard to sit still, made it hard to *breathe*. But his admission that he was at last going to face up to his past and not let it dominate his present made her feel like cheering.

'You won't take the credit for anything, will you? I've never met a woman so generous of spirit that she would not dent a man's fragile ego by proving *she* was the one who saw things much more clearly than he did. It makes me think that I should hold onto you, Grace…yes hold onto you and never let you go.'

As well as making her heart race with joy, his sincere assertion sent her emotions into a tailspin. She yearned to tell him there and then that she loved him, but first she had to tell him about the abrupt change to her plans…

'Marco?'

'Yes, Grace?'

'I don't know how to cushion this, but I'm afraid I need to go back to Africa…to the orphanage.'

'When?' He instantly removed his sunglasses, and she was sure she didn't imagine the shadow that moved across his irises. 'You're not telling me you plan on going soon? Not before our holiday is ended?'

Her tongue came out to moisten her suddenly dry lips. 'I'm afraid I am. I'm going to have to go today, in fact. Two of the workers at the home have contracted a fever and are being treated in hospital. That leaves only two other people to help care for the children. They're desperately short-handed, and there's nobody else that can go other than me... All the charity's field-workers are already working abroad elsewhere—plus I know the children, and they know me. As well as needing practical help, they'll need reassuring that everything's going to be all right.'

His face darkened, and she bit down on her lip. The duck-egg-blue sky suddenly didn't seem quite so blue or benign... 'It's not that I don't *want* to stay with you, Marco...it's just that this is an emergency. I have no choice but to respond to the charity's request for my help.'

He rose to his feet and strode over to the edge of the balcony, to stare out at the shimmering verdant lawns of the golfing resort in the distance. *The scene of where they had first met...*

Grace got slowly up from her chair to join him, unable to ignore the stiffening of the broad shoulders encased in his black fitted shirt that told her he was already shutting her out emotionally because of what he must no doubt see as a betrayal.

Marco turned round to face her. The shadows in his deep dark eyes made her heart sink like a boulder. 'How do you expect me to feel? I know how much you care about others, Grace, but what about yourself? You are supposed to be resting—recovering from the exhaustion you suffered after your last visit. And most of all I don't want you to put your own health at risk by going out there while a fever is raging. Didn't you already tell me that the baby Azizi died from it? How on earth could I be happy about you returning there now?'

Flushing, Grace dipped her head. 'We don't even know yet if what the workers have contracted is the same fever that killed Azizi. It could be a completely different strain altogether…a less virulent one. The hospital lab will have to run some tests. The most important thing is that those poor, defenceless children shouldn't be left without help and support. I know I was exhausted when I came back from there, but I'm strong and in good health. I'll be absolutely fine…I know I will,' she added, feeling the helpless sting of tears behind her eyes because Marco had made it abundantly clear that not only would he not consider going with her, but his tone also suggested that she was crazy for even contemplating making such a trip.

'I don't want you to go.' Scrubbing his hand round his jaw, he moved his head a little despairingly from side to side. 'I know you'll probably go anyway…after all, it's what you're all about, isn't it? Helping those less fortunate, I mean. It's commendable to be so dedicated, but being dedicated is one thing—risking life and limb is another!'

'I'm sorry, Marco…but you're right. I *am* going. Try not to think too badly of me for it.'

'I don't think badly of you…I *couldn't*. But I still wish that you'd reconsider.'

Even though she couldn't be sure that everything would be all right, Grace knew that she must still go. Her strong natural instinct to help was too compelling to ignore, so she would answer it—if only to assure herself that everything humanly possible would be done to aid the children.

Looking as though he'd wanted to say more to persuade her to stay, but had concluded that he wouldn't, Marco turned away and strode across the sunlit patio to the open French doors that led back into the living room. It hit her then that he was leaving, and that it might be a long time before she saw him again. A scalding tear slid down her cheek that their relationship should take such an unhappy turn.

'Marco? Please don't let's part on bad terms. I promise I'll be okay. Can you wait just a minute?'

Flying across to the table, she picked up the notepad and pen she'd left lying there, with which she'd been making notes about her trip back to Africa. She scribbled down her mobile phone number, along with her address back in the UK. As an afterthought, she wrote down her parents' phone number and address too.

Tearing out the page from the notepad, she moved quickly across to where Marco was waiting and handed it to him. 'If you want or need to contact me, then you should have this.'

He slowly nodded his head, took the sheet of notepaper and slid it into the back pocket of his jeans. 'Have your flights been booked already?'

'Yes. The charity has arranged everything. A cab is coming soon to take me to the airport.'

'Are you okay for money?'

'Yes…I'm fine.'

'Then there is nothing more to say, is there? Nothing except take care of yourself—and don't take any more risks than you strictly need to.'

There was a husky catch in his voice that made Grace fleetingly hold her breath. Then, leaning forward to cup her face, he kissed her hard, almost bruising her lips with the passionate pressure of his mouth. Before she could gather her wits—and without so much as a backward glance—he turned and walked away. Seconds later she heard the front door slam resoundingly…

CHAPTER TWELVE

THE rain hit the concrete pavements hard, bouncing up on impact like thin, pointed daggers. Although it might be deemed refreshing, after the dry burning heat he had left behind in the Algarve, Marco felt too bleak to mind whether it rained or it didn't. As he stared out of the windows of the Mercedes at the unfamiliar suburban streets he'd never had reason to visit up until now his mouth dried, and his heart pounded at the prospect of seeing Grace again after six interminably long weeks. He felt bleak because his separation from her had been like a death sentence. It had worn him down, prevented him from concentrating at work, and made him snarl like a tiger every time something didn't go his way...

Although he'd rung her mobile several times it had been to no avail. Trying desperately hard not to let his fearful imagination run away with him, he'd followed up the futile calls with several to the charity in London, whose number he'd found out when Grace and he had first met, but the manager there had been frustratingly close-mouthed about how Grace was faring, refusing even to tell him when she might be returning home again because he wasn't family.

Marco had hated that. He'd wanted to yell at them that he fully intended to *be* her family, if she'd have him. But he hadn't said that. Instead he'd rung her parents' number and spoken to her father—Peter. He was the one who had told him haltingly that Grace had been taken ill at the orphanage, after practically working herself into the ground, and that after spending a week in hospital she was being flown home to London... In fact, he'd been about to fly over there to travel back with her.

That had been over a week ago now. Peter Faulkner had advised Marco to wait awhile before visiting his daughter—'at least a week'—because when she got home she would need some time to acclimatise and recover her strength before having visitors.

It had been another test of gargantuan endurance to wait for a week, not knowing if Grace's health was improving or not. Marco had been to hell and back in fear that she might not make it—that she wouldn't recover and might die before he got the chance to tell her how much she meant to him... So now, as Miguel drove the car onto the generously wide drive of a smart detached red-brick house at the end of a tree-lined avenue, Marco dropped his head into his hands and murmured a fervent prayer.

When he'd lifted his head he flexed his hands several times, because they were clammy with fear at how he might find Grace. At the back of his mind was the memory of Miguel confiding in him that the love of his life had died from a terminal disease. *Why, oh, why had he not agreed to fly out to Africa with her?* If only he had been able to get over the sense that she was abandoning him—even though he'd known what she was doing was *beyond* courageous and deserved nothing but his admiration and respect. But, in his defence, her change of plans had devastated him.

'Deus!'

'We are here, Senhor Aguilar.' Miguel opened the passenger door and held a large black umbrella over Marco's head as he stepped out onto the smartly paved drive.

The man who had become a true friend to him over the past weeks, since Grace had departed for Africa, briefly proffered a smile. Contained in that friendly gesture was a wealth of empathy and understanding at what Marco must be going through.

'I will wait in the car,' he said respectfully as Marco nervously tunnelled his fingers through his hair, then ran his hand down over the sleeve of his chocolate-coloured suede jacket.

'Thank you.' Accepting the umbrella to shield himself from the still torrential rain, he turned away to press the button that rang the doorbell on the house's scarlet-painted front door.

After briefly introducing himself to Grace's serious-faced but amiable father, he followed the silver-haired older man through a spotlessly neat living room out to a glass conservatory, where he told Marco that Grace was resting.

Marco sucked in a breath to steady himself when he saw her. She was sitting perfectly still in a rattan rocking chair that was pulled up close to the clear plate-glass windows, staring out at the sheeting rain that hammered dramatically onto the garden as though transfixed. Her pretty blonde hair had been left loose to fall softly round her shoulders and appeared to be a little longer. She was wearing a thin white sweater with denim jeans, and her small hands were clutching the wooden arms of her chair as if to anchor herself, he saw. She put him in mind of a fragile porcelain figure set on a mantelshelf—one false move would send it crashing to the ground to splinter into a thousand tiny pieces that would be near impossible to put together again.

The icy shard of fear that sliced through him made him feel almost physically sick.

'Grace?' Peter Faulkner moved up behind his daughter to lay a gentle hand on her shoulder. 'You've got a visitor, love.'

'Who is it?' At the same time that she asked the question she turned her head, and her startled cornflower-blue gaze collided with Marco's. 'Oh, my God…'

It was too quiet and too stunned to be an exclamation, but even as he registered the words Marco saw that his appearance had deeply affected her. Likewise, the sight of her staggered him.

'I tried to ring you so many times—' he started, but emotion hit him with all the force of a rogue wave he hadn't anticipated, scrambling the thoughts in his head so emphatically that he scarce knew what to say. There was so much he wanted to communicate, but where to begin?

He cleared his throat, moving a little closer to where she sat. Out of the corner of his eye he saw her father lean over and drop an affectionate kiss on the top of her head.

'I think I'll leave you two to get reacquainted. When you're ready, your mum will make us all a nice cup of tea.'

'Thanks, Dad.'

Grace waited until her father had vacated the room and shut the door behind him before she turned her face up to Marco's and gave him a smile. The gesture was no less dazzling than it had always been, even though she looked far more fragile than when he had last seen her.

'I can't believe that you're here,' she said softly.

'What have you been doing to yourself? You've lost weight, and you don't look well at all.' He bit back the despairing anger that suddenly gripped him, frustrated that he no longer seemed able to contain the great swell of emotion that washed over him at even the thought of Grace.

'I just need some rest to help me get my strength back, then I'll be fine.'

'That's what you told me the last time we were to-gether... "I'll be fine," you said. Now I see that you're not. I should *never* have let you leave.'

'Marco?'

With a tender smile that he didn't feel he deserved at all, she reached for his hand to enfold it in hers. His heart missed a beat, and when he answered his voice was a little gruff. 'What?'

'I'm so glad you came to see me. I—I was afraid you might forget me.'

'Are you crazy?'

Mindful of her weakened state, he carefully but firmly pulled her up from the chair and embraced her, clutch-ing her to his chest as if terrified she was a mere figment of his fevered imagination that might vanish at any sec-ond. But the reality that he *was* holding her in his arms again made him feel as if he might die from the sheer pleasure and relief of it, even though at the back of his mind he registered worriedly that her bones had far less flesh covering them than they'd used to. *Had she eaten at all in six long weeks?*

Pressing his lips against her soft wheat-coloured hair, he breathed in the scent of the silken skeins as if they were anointed with the most divine scent a master per-fumer could devise. 'Could I forget the moon and stars...

the sun or the sky? To me, my angel, you are all those combined and *more*.'

When Grace pulled back a little and turned her face up to his Marco saw that her incomparable blue eyes were drowned in tears.

'Baby, don't cry… It near kills me to see you cry,' he soothed, cupping her face.

'I'm only crying because I'm so happy that you're here.'

Intent on stealing just a short, affectionate kiss, so as not to overwhelm her, Marco changed his mind the instant he felt her satin-soft lips quiver beneath his. He ravished her mouth with a heartfelt helpless groan. When he realised that Grace was kissing him back with equally as much ardour and passion, some of the fear that had dogged him since he'd heard she had been taken ill ebbed away. As if by mutual silent agreement they slowed the tenor of the caress so that gradually it became tender rather than passionate.

Marco lifted his head to observe her with a rueful smile. 'I too am very happy to be here, Grace. I've been like a wounded bear since you left, and not fit company for anyone. But tell me…how was it that you never answered your phone? As I said before, I tried to contact you on numerous occasions while you were away.'

She emitted a soft, regretful sigh. 'I'm afraid I lost my mobile the day after I arrived in Africa, and once at the orphanage I just didn't have the time or energy to source another one. That's why you couldn't reach me. But I swear I thought about you every day, Marco. Every spare moment that I had—and there weren't many—I thought of you. I shouldn't have rushed away like I did.'

She paused to brush away the tears that dampened her cheek, and her lower lip trembled.

'I mean...they needed me at the orphanage, but I was still exhausted from my last trip out there and I felt the effects almost straight away. Because we were so short-staffed the situation was almost unbearable at times. Perhaps I was arrogant, believing I could make a differ-ence...that I could help make the situation better in some way. The three of us working together using all of our wits and know-how...every *ounce* of our energy...could only just about hold it together. You'd better not accuse me of seeing things clearly again, because it's not true. If I'd listened to my body and not my heart I wouldn't have got sick.'

Tenderly stroking back the hair that brushed the sides of her face, Marco frowned. 'Listen to me. To do what you did was the bravest and most selfless thing I've ever heard, and I had no right to try and make you change your mind about going when we last saw each other. You weren't arrogant to believe you could make a differ-ence, and I'll wager if you asked any one of those chil-dren whether they felt safer and more secure because you were around not one of them would deny it. Talking of which—did any more children or staff go down with the fever? Apart from you, I mean?'

'One little girl of about four years old.' Grace gave a slight shake of her head, as if the memory pained her. 'But she was recovering well, thank God, by the time I was taken ill myself.'

'And what have the doctors said about your condition, hmm?' *He was almost afraid to ask in case the news was bad.* He could hardly attest to breathing as he anxiously waited for her reply.

'They've said that I'm suffering from both physical and nervous exhaustion. I didn't get the fever, thank God. But the heat out there sucked all the energy from me.

It didn't help matters that the resources and help were so inadequate, and caring for the children was much harder than usual. I'm afraid I lost my appetite completely, which was an added complication, and one morning I just passed out. When I came to I didn't have the strength to get up. My co-workers said I was muttering incomprehensible things and sounding delirious. Next thing I knew I was in the hospital. Anyway…all that's behind me now. Give me just a few more days of rest and relaxation and I'll be as right as rain, I'm sure.' She glanced over her shoulder at the bucketing rain that still poured, as if to confirm it to herself.

'Hmm.' Marco wasn't nearly so sure. The faint bruising smudges beneath her eyes and the haunted look they held told a rather *different* story.

'Are you planning on staying here in Britain for very long?' she asked him, her tone a little nervous.

'Do you imagine I am going to get on the next plane back to Portugal and leave you here while you are ill?'

'I don't know. I don't know *what* you plan to do. How could I?'

'You look like you're about to cry again. Does my being here distress you so much?'

She dropped her hand to his sleeve and laid it there. Marco was so sensitive to her every touch that he swore he felt her heat burn him right through to his bones, even through the thick suede of his jacket.

'I don't want you to go. I know it probably won't do me any good, telling you that. You've no doubt had enough of my ridiculous demands. And I'm so sorry if I tried to force you in any way to confront your past, like I was some kind of expert. I'm not. Sometimes I just get carried away with my desire to make everything right for everybody. It's crazy, I know.' She gave a tired smile. 'I guess I'm more like my parents than I realised.'

'It's not crazy to want to help. And you *did* help me by getting me to look at my past and not run away from it. You certainly didn't force me. Somehow being with you, having your own bravery as an example, I *wanted* to face my demons. I only wish there were more people like you in the world, Grace.'

'I'm not unique. I told you that before. Look…I know you're a very busy and important man, and you're probably anxious to get back to your work—wherever that might take you in the world—and I know I let you down, but I hope you can stay…for a little while at least.'

Marco took a deep breath in, then wiped the back of his hand across lips that were still throbbing from his and Grace's passionate kiss. 'I'm not going anywhere in a hurry…you can count on that. And you didn't let me down. You were fulfilling your dreams, that's all, and I can't be upset about that when I've always tried to fulfil my own. But nothing is more important to me right now than seeing that you're all right. What I've seen so far tells me that you're a long way from being fully recovered from your trip—so, like I said, I will not be doing anything other than staying here with you until you're well again. I've booked a room in a hotel nearby, so I can be on hand whenever you need me. Plus, you and I need to have a long talk about things. But first I would like to have a word with your father, if I may?'

Grace's blue eyes widened warily. 'What for?'

'I'd like to get an update from him about what your doctors have said. I'd also like to recommend one of my own doctors to look at you. I have access to the very best medical care in the world, Grace, and I'd like you to benefit from it—if you agree?'

She turned away, folding her arms across the thin white sweater that so starkly highlighted the fact she'd lost weight. 'You don't need to talk to my dad. I've already given you an update on my health. And nor do I need to see one of your doctors. I told you…I'll be fine.'

There *was* something wrong. Marco sensed it the moment she dipped her head and turned away. His mouth went dry as a desert plain. 'You're keeping something from me…what is it?'

'It's nothing.' All of a sudden she moved back to the rocking chair. Lowering herself down into the seat, she returned her hands to its polished wooden arms and started to rock herself slowly back and forth.

Outside, the rain thundered against the conservatory's glass roof, with no sign of letting up any time soon. Staring at her, Marco curled his hands into anxious fists down by his sides. 'If you won't tell me then I'll go and find your father and ask him.'

The chair stopped rocking, and the incandescent blue eyes couldn't hide her apprehension and fear. 'You don't need to go and find my dad. It's just that…when the doctors did all the usual tests on me in the hospital…something turned up that none of us expected.'

'If you have any idea of how much agony of mind I'm going through right now, then for God's sake *please* just come out with it and tell me!' Marco implored.

Holding her hand to her middle, as if a debilitating pain had just shot through her, Grace suddenly turned as pale as new milk. He was already moving to her side when she slumped forward in the chair in a dead faint.

'Grace, wake up! *Querido Deus!*' Crouching down in front of her, he gently positioned her so that she was sitting more securely in the chair, with her head dropped onto her chest. Quickly he felt for her pulse. His own was probably just as out of kilter in fear and concern.

He was just about to leap up and call for Grace's father to ring for an ambulance when she opened her eyes and stared at him in confused distress. 'Marco,' she murmured, 'what happened?'

'You fainted that's what happened, Grace. I think you should be in bed rather than sitting in here. Your hands are freezing!' Saying so, he took her pale, slender hands in his and vigorously rubbed them, as if to invigorate her blood once again and restore her to the land of the living.

His mind was running at a mile a minute in search of solutions that might help. No matter how much Grace pleaded with him not to, Marco fully intended to speak to her father about her condition, followed by consulting his own doctors. It was unbearable to imagine that she might be taken from him through illness when he'd so recently realised that he couldn't possibly live without her...

'I'm fine.'

'Stop saying that when it is clearly not the truth!' Breathing hard, Marco couldn't—*wouldn't*—take his eyes off her, in case she fainted again. 'Just before you passed out you were holding your stomach as if you were in pain. Are you hurting, Grace? If you need medical help then you must tell me.'

A wan smile briefly touched her lips. 'I wasn't in pain. I just felt a little nauseous, that's all. Can you pass me that glass of water on the table behind you? I'd like a sip.'

He did as she asked and quickly returned. As he watched her sip the water his mind careened in all directions, imagining all the dire reasons why she would be feeling nauseous.

Reaching forward, Grace put the glass carefully down

on the white ledge beside the conservatory doors. 'It's perfectly natural for a woman to feel nauseous sometimes when she's pregnant,' she announced, her tone unbelievably matter-of-fact, 'especially in the first three months.'

'What did you say?'

'I'm telling you that the reason I'm feeling nauseous is that I'm pregnant.'

Even the rain that thundered so powerfully against the roof couldn't drown out the enormous sense of shock and disbelief that rolled through Marco.

If she hadn't felt quite so weak just then Grace would have quickly reassured him that he needn't worry…she wasn't about to demand he marry her or anything crazy like that. There were plenty of women all around the world who raised their children on their own, and if he didn't want to be with her then that was what she would do.

The way his arresting features had turned almost pale beneath his bronzed skin had already told her that it was hardly welcome news. Now she wished she'd kept quiet about the pregnancy—at least until she felt strong enough to deal with the emotional fall-out should Marco tell her he was sorry but he didn't want to assume the responsibility of being a father, not on the kind of regular basis that a truly loving relationship required that he be…

But now, looking a little more recovered, he clasped her hands more tightly, his hooded dark eyes roving her face as if she was indeed the moon, the stars and the sun that he'd asserted that she was earlier.

'The child—the child is…' he started to say.

'Don't you *dare* ask me if it's yours,' Grace leapt in, feeling her cheeks flush with some much needed colour.

'I wouldn't dream of it.' His lips twisted with gentle mockery, then he stared at her in wonder, laying the flat of his palm gently against her abdomen. 'I'm going to be a father.'

'Yes, you are. Do you mind?'

'Do I *mind*?'

'You told me once that you didn't know what it meant to be a father because you'd had no good example of a father yourself.'

'That's true. But I never said I was averse to learning if the right woman came along, did I?'

Grace's heart skipped. 'Am *I* the right woman, then?'

'I thought you were clever... But if you still haven't worked it out yet, then I guess I will have to enlighten you, won't I?'

Staying silent, she minutely examined every curve and facet of his extraordinarily handsome face, wondering how she had lived for so long without the sight of it, yet still wary of having her longed-for treasure cruelly taken away if anything untoward should happen to either of them.

'For once you're lost for words.' Chuckling, Marco touched his fingertips to her lips and tenderly traced them. 'I love you, Grace. You have become the ground beneath my feet, the person by which I stand or fall, because I can't...I *won't* live without you. You're the most courageous, loving and loyal woman I have ever met.'

Grace's eyes had filled with tears the moment he'd said, 'I love you'. *Was she allowed to be this happy?* she wondered. When there was so much pain and sadness in the world, it was incredible that she should be blessed with so much joy, she thought gratefully. 'I love you too, Marco. I adore you more than you can ever know, and I promise to spend the rest of my life trying to show you just how much.'

'Are you two sufficiently reacquainted to have that

cup of tea now? Only you're mum's got her best china laid out in the dining room, and she's wearing a hole in the kitchen floor waiting to get the go-ahead.'

Her dad put his head round the door just as they were about to embrace passionately. Grace met Marco's melting brown eyes and giggled helplessly.

'If we can have just five minutes more, then *yes*. A cup of tea would be most welcome,' Marco murmured in her ear.

Before Grace had the chance to convey this to her dad, Marco moved his face closer. 'Marry me,' he whispered—just before his lips ardently claimed hers...

EPILOGUE

The VIP lounge at Heathrow was surprisingly quiet that morning. Apart from Grace, Marco and their six month old baby boy, Henry, there was a smart elderly couple and a striking lady dressed in the colourful full regalia of the African region she came from.

Their beautiful little son was already a veteran when it came to travelling. Marco wouldn't leave them at home whenever he had to travel abroad for work, and neither did Grace want him to. They'd been married for just over a year now, and she still couldn't bear to be apart from him—not even for a day.

Just a couple of months after Henry was born they'd flown back to Portugal, where her entrepreneur husband had been developing a golfing academy specifically for disadvantaged young men and women. And now, after a fortnight staying in their lovely new home in Kensington, they were at the airport again—this time to fly out to Africa and visit not only the newly erected orphanage, but also the on-site medical centre, staffed by highly trained professionals. Marco had had it set up and, they'd named it after Azizi.

She was so proud of her wonderful husband. Not only had he confronted his fears surrounding his past, he had transcended them to give his unstinting help to children raised in an orphanage just like him.

Their little son was fretting, and Grace rocked him in her arms to try and soothe him. Behind them the loud roar of a jumbo jet taking off drowned out any other sounds.

'I think his first tooth is coming through. He's been dribbling a lot, and he keeps sucking his fist,' she told her handsome husband anxiously. He was dressed as immaculately as ever, in an Italian tailored suit. Marco never failed to take her breath away with his striking appearance. But, expensive suit or not, he didn't hesitate to reach for his son.

'Give him to me. Why don't you go and sit down and relax for a while? Pour yourself some juice.'

'I wish I could have another cup of coffee. I didn't sleep much last night.'

'It's not a good idea to have too much coffee when you're breastfeeding, my angel. Remember what the paediatrician said?'

'I know. She said not to have more than three cups a day. I suppose I ought to save my quota until we board the plane, at least. No doubt it's going to be a long, tiring day.' Grace handed over the baby with a hard-to-suppress yawn.

Marco carefully nestled the infant in the crook of his arm and began to mimic the rocking motion that his wife regularly used to calm him or get him off to sleep.

Henry's still-blue eyes drifted closed immediately, and Grace shook her head in wonder. 'And you were worried about being a good father? You're a natural. You seem to have a magic touch where Henry's concerned.' She saw him flush a little beneath his tan, and he didn't need to tell her how proud of his son he was.

Wanting to take care of their newborn herself, she'd declined his offer of hiring a full-time nurse to help her. Yet when Henry woke up for his feed during the night it was Marco who leapt out of bed to fetch him and bring him to her. Then, after he'd fallen asleep again, he'd hold him for a long time—'father-and-son bonding time' he called it—before taking him back to his cot.

'Sometimes it's hard to believe how fortunate I am,' he said now. 'You and Henry have given me everything I ever dreamed of and more. For the first time when I say I'm going home I *mean* it. I love you with all my heart, my beautiful, clever girl.'

Leaning towards him, Grace stole a gently lingering kiss. The three other passengers in the lounge glanced at each other in approval. 'I love you too, my darling.' She smiled seductively. 'And I'll show you how much tonight—after we put Henry to bed,' she whispered.

His eyes gleamed with love and desire. 'If I wasn't holding our son, I wouldn't hesitate to demonstrate what I think about that, you little temptress!'

'Promises promises...' Grinning, Grace sashayed over to a luxurious leather armchair and sat down, knowing without any conceit at all that her husband's compelling dark eyes hungrily tracked her all the way...

* * * * *

Mills & Boon® Hardback

February 2012

ROMANCE

An Offer She Can't Refuse	Emma Darcy
An Indecent Proposition	Carol Marinelli
A Night of Living Dangerously	Jennie Lucas
A Devilishly Dark Deal	Maggie Cox
Marriage Behind the Façade	Lynn Raye Harris
Forbidden to His Touch	Natasha Tate
Back in the Lion's Den	Elizabeth Power
Running From the Storm	Lee Wilkinson
Innocent 'til Proven Otherwise	Amy Andrews
Dancing with Danger	Fiona Harper
The Cop, the Puppy and Me	Cara Colter
Back in the Soldier's Arms	Soraya Lane
Invitation to the Prince's Palace	Jennie Adams
Miss Prim and the Billionaire	Lucy Gordon
The Shameless Life of Ruiz Acosta	Susan Stephens
Who Wants To Marry a Millionaire?	Nicola Marsh
Sydney Harbour Hospital: Lily's Scandal	Marion Lennox
Sydney Harbour Hospital: Zoe's Baby	Alison Roberts

HISTORICAL

The Scandalous Lord Lanchester	Anne Herries
His Compromised Countess	Deborah Hale
Destitute On His Doorstep	Helen Dickson
The Dragon and the Pearl	Jeannie Lin

MEDICAL

Gina's Little Secret	Jennifer Taylor
Taming the Lone Doc's Heart	Lucy Clark
The Runaway Nurse	Dianne Drake
The Baby Who Saved Dr Cynical	Connie Cox

Mills & Boon® Large Print
February 2012

ROMANCE

The Most Coveted Prize	Penny Jordan
The Costarella Conquest	Emma Darcy
The Night that Changed Everything	Anne McAllister
Craving the Forbidden	India Grey
Her Italian Soldier	Rebecca Winters
The Lonesome Rancher	Patricia Thayer
Nikki and the Lone Wolf	Marion Lennox
Mardie and the City Surgeon	Marion Lennox

HISTORICAL

Married to a Stranger	Louise Allen
A Dark and Brooding Gentleman	Margaret McPhee
Seducing Miss Lockwood	Helen Dickson
The Highlander's Return	Marguerite Kaye

MEDICAL

The Doctor's Reason to Stay	Dianne Drake
Career Girl in the Country	Fiona Lowe
Wedding on the Baby Ward	Lucy Clark
Special Care Baby Miracle	Lucy Clark
The Tortured Rebel	Alison Roberts
Dating Dr Delicious	Laura Iding

Mills & Boon® Hardback

March 2012

ROMANCE

Roccanti's Marriage Revenge	Lynne Graham
The Devil and Miss Jones	Kate Walker
Sheikh Without a Heart	Sandra Marton
Savas's Wildcat	Anne McAllister
The Argentinian's Solace	Susan Stephens
A Wicked Persuasion	Catherine George
Girl on a Diamond Pedestal	Maisey Yates
The Theotokis Inheritance	Susanne James
The Good, the Bad and the Wild	Heidi Rice
The Ex Who Hired Her	Kate Hardy
A Bride for the Island Prince	Rebecca Winters
Pregnant with the Prince's Child	Raye Morgan
The Nanny and the Boss's Twins	Barbara McMahon
Once a Cowboy...	Patricia Thayer
Mr Right at the Wrong Time	Nikki Logan
When Chocolate Is Not Enough...	Nina Harrington
Sydney Harbour Hospital: Luca's Bad Girl	Amy Andrews
Falling for the Sheikh She Shouldn't	Fiona McArthur

HISTORICAL

Untamed Rogue, Scandalous Mistress	Bronwyn Scott
Honourable Doctor, Improper Arrangement	Mary Nichols
The Earl Plays With Fire	Isabelle Goddard
His Border Bride	Blythe Gifford

MEDICAL

Dr Cinderella's Midnight Fling	Kate Hardy
Brought Together by Baby	Margaret McDonagh
The Firebrand Who Unlocked His Heart	Anne Fraser
One Month to Become a Mum	Louisa George

Mills & Boon® Large Print
March 2012

ROMANCE

The Power of Vasilii	Penny Jordan
The Real Rio D'Aquila	Sandra Marton
A Shameful Consequence	Carol Marinelli
A Dangerous Infatuation	Chantelle Shaw
How a Cowboy Stole Her Heart	Donna Alward
Tall, Dark, Texas Ranger	Patricia Thayer
The Boy is Back in Town	Nina Harrington
Just An Ordinary Girl?	Jackie Braun

HISTORICAL

The Lady Gambles	Carole Mortimer
Lady Rosabella's Ruse	Ann Lethbridge
The Viscount's Scandalous Return	Anne Ashley
The Viking's Touch	Joanna Fulford

MEDICAL

Cort Mason – Dr Delectable	Carol Marinelli
Survival Guide to Dating Your Boss	Fiona McArthur
Return of the Maverick	Sue MacKay
It Started with a Pregnancy	Scarlet Wilson
Italian Doctor, No Strings Attached	Kate Hardy
Miracle Times Two	Josie Metcalfe